The Full Story

Dawn Stewardson

TORONTO • NEW YORK • LONDON
AMSTERDAM • PARIS • SYDNEY • HAMBURG
STOCKHOLM • ATHENS • TOKYO • MILAN • MADRID
PRAGUE • WARSAW • BUDAPEST • AUCKLAND

ISBN 0-373-71175-1

THE FULL STORY

This edition published by arrangement with Harlequin Books S.A.

Visit us at www.eHarlequin.com

Printed in U.S.A.

"There's a hit man trying to kill Billy Brent."

There was a short silence before Mickey continued speaking into her cell phone. "It'll be the mother of all stories and we'll have an exclusive. We'll scoop the *Chronicle* and the *Examiner*. Hell, we'll scoop the *New York Times*."

She lapsed into silence, obviously listening to whatever her boss was saying. Dan felt his blood pressure rising. He wished he could hear both sides of the conversation.

"I know I'm not the best candidate." She was speaking again. "But the critical thing is I'm up here with Dan O'Neill, and I'm the only person he's willing to take along."

Willing to take along? That was hardly the way he'd put it. There was another silence, and Dan couldn't keep himself from whispering, "Is he going for it?"

She smiled at him. "I'm on hold. He's running it past the editor in chief."

Dan held his breath. Surely an editor in chief would recognize the insanity of this.

And then Mickey said, "That's great. Tell Mr. Edwards I'll come through. Neither of you will be disappointed."

Dammit. Dan should have realized how persuasive she could be. After all, she'd convinced him to go along with this ridiculous scheme.

Dear Reader,

For my January 2003 Harlequin Superromance novel, *Finding Amy*, I created a company called Risk Control International—which turned out to have so many exciting people working for it that Harlequin will be publishing a miniseries of stories featuring various RCI operatives.

According to its director, RCI is in the "survival business," a phrase he prefers over saying that people come to RCI because their lives are in danger. The only rule the company has is "Don't let the client get killed," and in *The Full Story* the client is Hollywood superstar Billy Brent.

A contract killer is after Billy, and it's up to RCI's personal security advisor, Daniel O'Neill, to keep Billy alive while learning who the hit man is and who's paid him to whack Billy.

However, Dan's plan for doing that runs into trouble when photojournalist Mickey Westover appears on the scene.

She's arrived to interview Billy, but when she discovers that his life is in jeopardy she realizes a front-page story has fallen straight into her lap—and she has no intention of letting it go, despite the fact that Dan O'Neill is bound and determined to be rid of her. And the sooner the better.

Sparks fly between Mickey and Dan from beginning to end, and I hope you enjoy the way their romance is spiced with both humor and danger.

Warmest wishes,

Dawn Stewardson

To John, always.

Books by Dawn Stewardson

HARLEQUIN SUPERROMANCE

329—VANISHING ACT
355—DEEP SECRETS
383—BLUE MOON
405—PRIZE PACKAGE
409—HEARTBEAT
432—THREE'S COMPANY
477—MOON SHADOW
498—ACROSS THE MISTY
521—COLD NOSES, WARM KISSES
551—ONCE UPON A CRIME
571—THE YANKEE'S BRIDE
615—GONE WITH THE WEST
653—BIG LUKE, LITTLE LUKE
691—SULLY'S KIDS
719—LOOKING FOR MR. CLAUS
748—WILD ACTION
795—THE WANT AD
827—MIXED MESSAGE
861—FALLING FOR THE ENEMY
909—CLOSE NEIGHBORS
947—THE MAN BEHIND THE BADGE
993—HIS CHILD OR HERS?
1048—UNEXPECTED OUTCOME
1107—FINDING AMY

CHAPTER ONE

THE MOUNTAINS OF Vancouver Island were home to some of the biggest trees Mickey had ever seen, and the air smelled so heavenly that she was driving with the windows down. Imagining herself a thousand miles from civilization was no challenge at all—until she reached her destination.

Then she was treated to a reality check. An eight-foot wrought-iron fence and a sign that read:

Private Property
No Hunting
Trespassers Will Be Prosecuted

Hmm. That certainly got the point across. And it was probably a lot more likely to discourage potential intruders than the fence. If it had razor wire it would give people pause, but as things stood it didn't look like an insurmountable obstacle.

She pulled up to the intercom speaker and said, "I'm here to see Mr. Brent."

There was no response, although she was sure she'd found the right place. According to Billy, the road dead-ended at his property. And this was clearly the end of the line.

After combing her fingers through her hair, she climbed out of the rental to check the gate—and wasn't at all surprised when she found it locked, even though the risk of riffraff banging on Billy Brent's door had to be minimal up here.

When a second attempt to rouse someone via the speaker failed, she tried a couple of honks on the horn. That did no good, either. So what was her next move?

Glancing at her cellular, she wished Billy had entrusted her with his number. Then she could simply phone to say she'd arrived. But since she couldn't do that, there seemed to be only one option left.

She absently rubbed her palms across her jeans, thinking she'd feel better about the idea of climbing over the gate and hiking down the driveway if she didn't know that Billy had a hundred acres here. Or if she could see exactly how far his hideaway was from the road.

For all she knew the drive was miles long, winding its way through forest that looked just as dense inside the fence as outside.

Her gaze drifted uneasily back to the sign.

No Hunting obviously implied there were things to hunt. And since she'd been warned that the woods were full of bears and cougars, she wasn't thinking in terms of bunny rabbits.

Still, surely the odds of becoming some animal's

lunch weren't very high. So she'd simply be glad the sign's third line didn't read Trespassers Will Be Shot.

And that there wasn't a fourth one saying Even Expected Visitors Are At Risk.

She wouldn't have been shocked by either. Billy's retreat might be in Canada, where the gun laws were strict, but he had a reputation for disregarding laws. He apparently fancied himself this generation's Clint Eastwood, and she'd heard that he had trouble preventing his screen roles from blurring into his real life.

Of course, he was such hot box office that there was always someone to bail him out of trouble. Otherwise, if even a quarter of the stories about his antics were true, his current residence would be prison.

She tucked her cell phone into her purse and got out of the car, then retrieved her camera bag from the trunk and considered whether she should take anything else with her.

Billy had specified no tape recorder, and her laptop wasn't always essential for this type of interview; often the notebook she kept with her camera was enough. And it didn't make sense to overload herself when she had a gate to climb and heaven only knows how far to walk.

Deciding that if she *did* need the computer she could always come back for it, she stashed her purse in the trunk, next to her carry-on. After locking up, she slung the camera bag over her shoulder and told herself to get moving. She had an appointment to keep.

Besides, she thought with a final glance at the sign, a moving target was harder to hit.

Trying not to imagine Billy Brent lurking on his porch with an AK-47, she clambered over the gate—having been a tomboy had left her with numerous handy skills—and started down the driveway. She'd only walked about a hundred feet before a couple of crows went into scream mode overhead.

Seized by the horrible feeling that they were yelling, "Watch out for the bear," she picked up her pace. A second later she was tackled from behind.

She landed facedown in the dirt and dizzy from the impact, with someone straddling her and pressing what had to be a gun against the back of her head.

Her life didn't flash before her, but the fear sweeping through her was so strong she figured cardiac arrest was imminent. Before she could make her voice work, her assailant said, "Just lie still while I check for weapons. Then I'll let you up."

Okay. Take a slow, deep breath and try to reduce the amount of adrenaline rushing through her. As terrified as she felt, he'd sounded so matter-of-fact that she probably wasn't a mere instant away from death. He was more likely Billy's bodyguard than a crazed mountain man, which meant she'd be okay. Except for the humiliation of his patting her down.

She gritted her teeth as he ran one hand thoroughly over her body—while keeping the gun to her head with the other.

Evidently satisfied that she was clean, he reached

over to where her camera case had landed beside her and began rummaging through its contents.

"If you broke my Nikon..." she muttered into the ground.

"It's fine, but you're lucky I didn't break your neck. You're trespassing."

He pushed himself up, then grabbed the back of her belt and hauled her to her feet.

"Who are you?" he demanded, placing his hands firmly on her shoulders and turning her around to face him. "And what are you doing here?"

She hated being manhandled, and the urge to kick him in the shin was almost uncontrollable. However, since his gun looked even bigger than it had felt, she settled for merely scowling at him while she brushed half a pound of dirt and pine needles off herself.

He scowled right back, his eyes the color of cold blue steel and filled with suspicion. But growing up with three older brothers had taught her everything she needed to know about glaring contests, so she stood her ground and sized the guy up.

He was somewhere in his mid-thirties, with dark hair that was far too short for her taste.

And he wasn't exceptionally tall—only about an even six feet.

As for his face, he had a crescent shaped scar above his upper lip that she'd guess had been carved by a knife. Aside from that, he resembled a young Richard Gere. Sort of. A young Richard Gere with a marine haircut.

In fact, Mr. Scar-face probably wouldn't be bad

looking if he smiled. And if his eyes held even a hint of warmth.

"I asked who you are," he reminded her at last.

He'd stuck the gun into the waistband of his jeans, but he still wasn't exhibiting the slightest trace of friendliness. So if she had any hope of actually getting to see Billy, she'd better try being at least reasonably pleasant.

"My name's Michelle Westover," she told him. "*Mickey* Westover."

"To your *friends,*" he said, his tone suggesting that wasn't what *he'd* be calling her.

"Yes. To my friends."

She forced a smile, then bent to retrieve her camera bag and checked her camera. It really *did* seem okay.

"And you're here because...?"

"Mr. Brent is expecting me."

"Yeah?"

She nodded. "I have an appointment."

"Oh?"

"I made it a week ago. I called his agent, his agent contacted him, and Mr. Brent phoned me. I gather he didn't mention anything about it to you?"

"That's right. So why don't you tell me *why* you're here to see him."

"And who would I be telling?" she said, trying not to let the question sound too snotty.

"I'm Dan O'Neill. An associate of Mr. Brent's."

"A bodyguard-type associate?"

He shrugged. "Something like that. So this appointment is to...?"

The man was focused, she'd give him that.

"I'm a photojournalist with *The San Francisco Post.* The Arts and Entertainment section. We've been running a series called *Hideouts of the Stars,* and Mr. Brent agreed to an interview."

O'Neill eyed her for a moment. "If you do a spread on somebody's hideout...doesn't that kind of defeat the purpose of having one?"

That was exactly what she'd initially thought, but since the party line was that everything the *Post*'s senior editors decided on made perfect sense, she merely said, "We never get specific about exactly where a place is—just publish photographs of it along with an article based on the interview."

O'Neill still seemed skeptical, but all he said was, "I'll have to see some ID."

"I left my purse in the car. Locked in the trunk," she elaborated when his expression suggested that only an idiot would leave her purse in a car.

But what was he thinking might happen to it out here in the wilderness? That a deer would lift it and take a trip to Mexico on one of her credit cards?

He didn't tell her what he was thinking, just said, "Let's go," and started off toward the gate.

She followed along, unable to force the cliché—a lean, mean, fighting machine—from her mind.

His shoulders were ridiculously broad, and the way his T-shirt pulled tautly across his back left no doubt that there were a whole lot of muscles beneath the black cotton.

Yes, she had to give him points for being in good shape. And for his voice.

It was nice and deep, with a barely there drawl that was just enough to make her sure he'd grown up somewhere in the South. She doubted he ever got accused of being a Southern gentleman, though.

He didn't strike her as a ladies' man—almost definitely not married and probably didn't even have a serious girlfriend. Her intuition about that sort of thing was seldom wrong, and his body language clearly said *loner.*

But what did she care about any of that? All she cared about was getting past this guy to Billy Brent.

AFTER MICKEY WESTOVER took her purse from the trunk, Dan checked every piece of ID that she had, ignoring the way she was doing a poor job of concealing her annoyance. That done, he had a careful second look at both her driver's license and her *Post* staff card.

The pictures on them definitely matched the woman—long hair the color of a good cigar, big brown eyes, Julia Roberts lips. And nothing else in her wallet was obviously phony. However, any self-respecting killer would carry top-quality fakes. And since the only visitor he'd been expecting, aside from a courier, was the person out to whack Billy…

He'd assumed it would be a man. But, hey, this was the twenty-first century. There were more and more hit women out there all the time. And Mickey Westover—if that really was her name—could easily be one of them.

Or maybe she was a forerunner for the killer. Sent to check the lay of the land and report back.

But, hell, every now and then his suspicions got the better of him and this was probably one of those times. Most likely, she was exactly who she claimed to be and Billy just hadn't thought to mention their appointment.

He might not even have remembered making it. With Billy, you could never be sure what he'd deposited in his memory bank and what had just slipped on by it.

"So?" Mickey said. "You're satisfied I'm legit?"

"Uh-huh. Regardless of that, though, Mr. Brent isn't here right now."

"Then why," she said, gesturing toward the wallet he was still holding, "have we been playing this little ID game?"

She was so clearly pissed off and trying not to show it that he almost laughed.

Resisting the impulse, he handed over her wallet and said, "I had to be sure who you were—whether Mr. Brent was here or not."

"Yes. Of course," she said, sticking the wallet back into her purse. "And at least, now, you'll be a step ahead when he gets back."

She stood watching him after she'd finished speaking, looking more suspicious by the second and finally saying, "He *will* be getting back, won't he?"

Damn. He couldn't say no. With everyone from Billy's agent to his PR handler claiming that he was up in Canada, enjoying a little time at his island retreat, if he admitted the man wasn't here at all…

Well, he could just imagine how Mickey Westover's cute little journalistic nose would start to quiver.

But if he told her Billy *would* be back, he'd bet that she'd want to wait right here for him.

"Look," he said at last. "He won't be home until late. And you've got a long drive from here back to…I assume you're staying in Victoria?"

"That's where I stayed last night. But I checked out of my hotel this morning, thinking I'd be flying back to San Francisco tonight. I can't go home without the interview, though," she added quickly.

"No, of course not. So let's play things this way. I'll wait up for Billy and we'll reschedule your appointment. And you can find a motel that's a lot closer than Victoria. Then, if you call me first thing in the morning, I'll tell you what time to be here." Dan did his best to look sincere even though what he'd really do, come morning, was tell her that Billy had changed his mind, had decided he didn't want pictures of this place in any newspaper.

After that, if she was the real thing she'd get on a plane and head home. And if she wasn't the real thing…well, he certainly knew what he'd do then.

"I don't suppose there's any way I could wait here for him," she finally said, just as he'd known she would.

"Sorry," he told her, trying to sound as if he really meant it. "But Mr. Brent's liable to be *very* late. And the thought of an overnight guest he's never even met... There are some things he just doesn't go for."

"I understand," she murmured.

He watched her climb into her car and set her purse and camera bag on the passenger seat, surprised that she was giving up so easily.

Apparently she didn't have the bulldog tenacity of most reporters, which probably explained why she got handed dumb assignments like...what had she said the series was called?

Oh, yeah, *Hideouts of the Stars.* Not much doubt she wouldn't be winning a Pulitzer for that one.

It was just as well she wasn't tenacious, though. The sooner she was gone and he could get back to those monitor screens—and resume watching for the *real* killer—the better.

He waited while she turned the car around. Then she gave him a little wave as she started off.

No hard feelings, it seemed to say.

But that wasn't what she'd be thinking come morning, when he told her there wouldn't be any interview.

MICKEY HEADED back toward the Trans-Canada Highway, which struck her as a grandiose name for a twisty-turny, two-lane mountain road. On the drive up here, she'd wondered several times what the secondary highways must be like.

At any rate, she drove more than far enough from Billy's hideaway to insure that the sound of her engine had faded from Mr. Dan O'Neill's range of hearing. Then she pulled over.

The man hadn't been straight with her.

She wasn't sure exactly what clue she'd picked up on. There'd been nothing in those cold blue eyes of his to tip her off.

But she was certain he'd been lying. And since her sixth sense seldom failed her, she suspected that Billy Brent was actually right there in his retreat. Exactly where he was supposed to be.

So had he simply changed his mind about the interview and told his bodyguard to get rid of her?

The more she considered the possibility, the more convinced she grew that that was precisely what had happened.

Billy wasn't known for his concern about others. The fact that she'd flown all the way up from San Francisco, then risked her life on a killer of a road, wouldn't count for diddly with him.

But he'd promised her an interview and she was damn well going to get one.

If she expected to ever be assigned serious stories, she had to come through on the lightweight ones. So, if Billy Brent *had* changed his mind, she'd just have to change it back.

The first step, though, would be getting to him without Daniel O'Neill intercepting her again. And how was she going to manage that?

Trying to march down the driveway a second time

was obviously out. And for all she knew there were surveillance cameras mounted in half the trees on Billy's property. So even if she avoided the driveway and made her way through the woods, O'Neill might spot her.

Besides, if she didn't stay within sight of the driveway she wouldn't know where she should be making her way *to*. Which would not be good.

Closing her eyes, she concentrated on trying to sketch a blueprint for action. When not a single good idea came to her, she opened her eyes again—and discovered that the god of happenstance was smiling down.

Heading along the narrow road toward her was a courier truck that had to be going to Billy's.

Well, actually it didn't have to be. She'd passed two or three private roads between the highway and his place. But she had a feeling that was where this truck was heading. So all she had to do was make the most of her chance.

After grabbing her purse and camera bag from the seat beside her, she rapidly climbed out of the car and waved at the driver—doing her best to act and think at the same time.

As he slowed to a stop, she offered up a little prayer that she could pull off a plan that had barely begun to germinate in her mind.

"Problem?" he said through his open window.

She did a half-second assessment and decided she had a good chance. His expression was one of fatherly concern.

"Yes," she said. "Definitely a problem. I turned off the highway just to see what was down here, but it's a dead end."

He nodded.

"Then, on the way back, my car died."

"Want me to look under the hood?"

"Thanks, but it's a rental and I've already called the roadside emergency number. There's a tow truck on the way, only..." She tried her hardest to look extremely frightened before adding, "I just saw a cougar."

"Really? You don't often spot them this time of day. Usually it's early morning or dusk."

Good Lord! He sounded as if cougar sightings were downright routine.

"Ah," she said. "Well, the thing is...seeing it scared me half to death and I'm afraid to stay here alone. So I wonder if I could catch a ride with you to a gas station or...anywhere there'd be people."

She waited, willing him to say "Sure."

Instead, he said, "As long as you sit tight inside your car you'll be just fine."

"I *can't,*" she said, unsuccessfully trying to produce a few tears. "I'm too frightened. I'm sorry to seem like such a wuss, but..."

The driver eyed her unhappily.

"I'll tell you what," he said at last. "There's a rule against picking up passengers. But if you wait here until I've made my delivery at the end of the road..."

Ah-ha! She'd *known* he was heading for Billy Brent's.

"What if I sat in back while you did the delivery?" she said. "Out of sight? I don't want to get you in any trouble, but if I have to stay here much longer by myself I'm going to start hyperventilating. I can feel it coming on."

The man looked even more unhappy; she tried the *willing* trick again.

"All right," he finally said. "Climb in."

"Oh, thank you so much!"

She took half a minute to retrieve her laptop from the trunk—if she ended up needing it, she wouldn't want to walk back all this way—then she got into the truck.

FROM HER POSITION in the back, Mickey heard Dan O'Neill say "Just a minute" not more than three seconds after the courier spoke into the intercom.

She assumed that the relatively friendly greeting, as opposed to being tackled and patted down at gunpoint, meant he'd been expecting this delivery.

The gate opened, creaking a little in the process, and the truck started forward again.

She quickly finished the note she'd been writing and read it over.

Dear Courier,

Thank you very much for the ride. I didn't want to inconvenience you any further, so I've gotten out.

I'll just tell these people that my car broke down and I walked here to wait for the emergency road service.

I won't breathe a word about your helping me, but I really appreciate it.

Your grateful passenger.

As the truck slowed to a stop, she snuck a peek out. And there was Billy Brent's retreat. Or rustic mansion might be more accurate.

It was a big, sprawling, one-story cedar thing—new trying to look old—with such a large brick chimney that she imagined the fireplace was enormous.

A porch ran along the front of the place, and she'd love to get a shot of Billy sitting in one of its carved rocking chairs. But first she had to find him.

She waited a few moments, until the driver was on his way to the front door, then slipped the note onto his seat, scooped up all her belongings from the floor and slid the passenger-side door open.

The instant her feet hit the ground, she scurried over to hide behind the nearest big tree.

From that vantage point, she watched Dan O'Neill sign for the delivery and the courier return to his vehicle.

He read her note, looked into the back, then simply put the truck in gear and drove off.

She remained where she was, giving O'Neill plenty of time to go back to whatever he'd been doing. When she figured he had, she took a deep breath, then dashed for the building and plastered herself against its front wall.

So far so good. That just left making her way around the perimeter and peering through windows until she spotted Billy.

He could hardly refuse to talk to her once she had him in her sights. At least she hoped he couldn't.

She started forward, but had only taken half a dozen steps before the silence was broken.

Her cell phone was ringing!

Frantically, she put the laptop and camera bag on the ground, then opened her purse and dug out the phone. Just as she was about to press the answer button so the stupid thing would shut up, O'Neill said, "Haven't we met before?"

Dammit to hell.

She turned toward the front door.

He was standing on the porch with his gun aimed at her once more.

CHAPTER TWO

MICKEY GAZED at Dan O'Neill and his gun, trying to think of something brilliant—or at least semi-intelligent—to say.

Before she could, he said, "Go ahead and answer your phone. I'll put my decision about whether to shoot you on hold."

She gave him a look to say she didn't find him even remotely amusing. Then, telling herself that in future she should think twice about sneaking into someplace where she knew an armed man was lurking, she pressed the phone's answer button and said, "Mickey Westover."

"Hi, it's Eric."

Terrific. Her boss. Who, an instant from now, would be asking how things were going.

"Hi," she said, trying to sound surprised but unperturbed. "What's up?"

"Oh, just calling to make sure you've connected with Billy Brent."

She glanced at Dan and felt a twinge of relief when she saw that he'd tucked the gun away, even though she was pretty sure he hadn't really been thinking about shooting her.

"We've almost connected," she told Eric. "I'm at his place and he's expected any minute now."

"But you haven't actually seen him."

"No, he was out when I got here."

"You *did* make a firm appointment, though."

"Yes. Of course."

When Eric didn't immediately reply, she couldn't stop her gaze from returning to Dan.

He rolled his eyes; she assumed it was the "expected any minute now" that he'd found a bit much.

As she pointedly turned her back on him, Eric said, "Mickey, I'm afraid this interview with Brent might have gone south."

"Pardon me?"

"Someone just told me that he's making an appearance on the Sherry Sherman Show tomorrow."

"What?"

"Apparently, she announced it this morning. And if he intends to be in New York for that, he's probably already on his way."

Oh, rats. Surely Eric's *someone* had misinformed him. Surely she hadn't missed the interview boat.

She turned toward Dan once more, gracing him with a grade A glare as she said, "Mr. Brent's associate assured me that he'd be here shortly. So let me just go check with him and I'll call you back, okay?"

"Okay. But make it fast."

"As fast as I can."

She clicked off, then said, "You're *certain* he'll be here tonight?"

"Uh-huh. Why?"

The man was lying to her again. Billy wasn't going to be here anytime in the near future.

He was en route to the Big Apple. And when she ended up home in San Francisco with no interview, she'd be so far into Eric's bad books that she'd never get out.

If the *Post* couldn't even count on her to file a story as mindless as this one, the next thing she knew she'd be kicked off Arts and Entertainment and assigned to writing obits. Assuming she still had a job at all.

But regardless of that, she wasn't about to let Mr. Dan O'Neill think he was getting away with something.

"You're absolutely positive," she said to him, "that Mr. Brent couldn't be…oh, maybe on his way to New York?"

Dan suddenly didn't look quite so self-assured, which made her feel a little better. Why should she be the only one who wasn't entirely happy?

"Oh his way to New York?" he repeated. "What would give you an idea like that?"

She watched his annoyance level rising while she made him wait before summarizing what Eric had told her.

"The Sherry Sherman Show," he said when she was done.

"Right. *Tomorrow morning's* Sherry Sherman Show. Which airs live on NBS at nine o'clock. *Eastern* time. So if you're seriously expecting him to show up here late tonight...well, the timing hardly works, does it?''

After eyeing her uneasily for a moment, Dan said, ''You wait right where you are. Don't move an inch,'' he added, heading for the house. ''I'll be back in a minute.''

DAN MARCHED INSIDE, telling himself that, regardless of what Mickey's boss had heard, Billy would *not* be appearing on any talk show in the morning. He'd be staying exactly where he was, holed up with Ken Heath in that sleepy little New England town they sometimes used on this sort of job.

Reaching the kitchen, he paused to scan the wall of surveillance monitors.

The retreat might have a rustic exterior, but its interior was filled with just about every modern luxury that had been invented—including state-of-the-art electronics. Cameras blanketed the entire area within a hundred yards of the house, and at the moment there was no movement out there.

For a couple of seconds, he let his gaze linger on Mickey Westover, who was still standing exactly where he'd left her.

Good. Everything was cool. And he likely had nothing to worry about as far as Billy was concerned. Not with Ken on the job.

He grabbed his phone from where he'd left it on the counter and punched in Ken's cellular number, thinking that the man was competence personified, the type who put one hundred percent into his assignments.

So since his current assignment was to keep Billy Brent under wraps, and not let the guy out of his sight, there was almost no chance of their star doing anything he shouldn't.

However, almost wasn't the same as no chance at all. And when it came to Billy, you just never knew.

The man was forty—probably older since you couldn't believe an actor's PR—but half the time he behaved like a fourteen-year-old. And although he probably wasn't crazy in certifiable terms, despite the fact that a lot of people might argue the point, he was definitely a loose cannon.

He seemed to come up with a hundred bizarre ideas a day, which meant that deciding to take off on his own, even though his life was in danger, would be just another in a long string of poor judgment calls.

With Ken keeping an eye on him, though, that should never have happened.

Dan was beginning to think Ken wasn't going to pick up when he finally did.

"It's O'Neill," Dan said. "Tell me that Brent's right there with you."

He let the silence last two seconds before saying, "Dammit, Ken, what's going on?"

There was another moment of dead air, then Ken said, "I'm in New York looking for him."

"Oh, shit." Why did Ken—Mr. Competence himself—have to pick now to screw up?

"Yeah, exactly," he was saying. "I'll find him, though. I was just hoping to do it before I had to tell you there was a problem."

"And he's planning to appear on national television in the morning?" Dan asked, hoping at least that part was wrong.

"You've got the entire story, then," Ken said.

So much for hoping.

"No, I'm sure I'm missing some," he said. "You'd better run the whole thing by me."

"Ah...yeah, okay. What happened was, he phoned Sherry Sherman last night. Apparently, they're buddies—go back to when he was on Broadway. She always used to have him as a guest then, so he could hype whatever show he was in. Which means he figures he owes her."

Dan silently began urging Ken to get on with it.

"At any rate," he continued at last, "when he called, she was upset because some big guest had just canceled. So our boy told her, no problem, he'd fill in."

"You aren't serious."

"'Fraid I am."

"Jeez, I don't believe it. He comes to us because his life's in danger, then turns around and agrees to be on national TV? What the hell does he figure the words *in hiding* mean?"

"Your guess is as good as mine. But his theory was that he'd just do the show and then drop out of sight again."

"It didn't occur to him that Sherry would announce he was going to be on? Give the killer a day's advance notice?''

"Well, to be fair, he didn't expect her to say anything. He assumed he'd be a surprise guest."

"Oh, sure. She's having one of the hottest stars in the galaxy on her show, and he didn't think she'd tell her viewers to tune in and see him?''

"Hell, Dan, who knows how the guy thinks?''

If he actually had to answer that question, he'd have to say he doubted *anyone* did. As far as he could tell, Billy's mental processes constituted a total enigma—and the only predictable thing about him was that he could be counted on to do the unpredictable.

Even so, going on TV when a killer was after him was crazy—even for Billy Brent.

"Anyhow," Ken continued, "after we'd discussed the fact that Sherry's little announcement made an appearance out of the question, Billy said he'd call her back and get himself out of it. Only the next thing I knew he'd taken a hike. Obviously changed his mind about reneging."

"So now he's wandering around New York. Ken, if—"

"Look, I'm going to find him. Worse comes to worst, I'll catch up with him when he arrives at the studio in the morning. Hustle him out of there and—"

"No, that just isn't good enough. If he shows his face anywhere near that studio he could end up dead. You've got to track him down today."

"That's what I'm *trying* to do. He told me a lot about what he does when he's in New York and I'm checking all his favorite haunts. I was only saying if worse comes to worst."

Dan drummed his fingers on the kitchen counter, thinking that Billy could be just about anywhere in the city. With just about anyone.

He'd performed in New York theaters for years before the megabucks of the movies had lured him to L.A. And he still spent a fair amount of time in Manhattan. Even referred to himself as "bi-coastal."

Which all added up to the fact that if Ken figured the odds on finding him today were good, he was deluding himself.

So what was the best move in light of that? Did it make more sense to stay put for the moment? Or should he head straight to New York and help Ken with his search?

Two people looking for Billy would be better than one. Yet if he left right now, he'd be forgoing his chance to wrap up this job if the killer *did* arrive at the retreat.

"Well?" Ken said.

"I'm thinking," he muttered.

Dammit, this wasn't one of his tougher assignments. At least, it shouldn't be. All he had to do was insure that Billy stayed alive and determine who wanted him dead.

And by far the simplest way to do that was to nail the hit man. Then, with a little persuasion, he'd convince the guy to reveal who'd hired him. But if he didn't nail the killer, the job could turn into something immensely more complicated.

Talking with Billy, he'd realized that there were a lot of people who might want the star dead—obviously, at least one of them badly enough to hire a contract killer.

Billy apparently alienated every second person he had much to do with, and alienated most of them pretty seriously. And then there was the greed factor.

The man was worth a gazillion bucks, even a small piece of which would be enough to keep most people happy for the rest of their lives. So between the motives of greed and revenge, and all the downright hatred…

He was getting off track, though.

The point was that if he could just get his hands on the killer, and make him say who'd hired him, none of the rest would matter.

Whereas, if he abandoned that plan, he'd have a whole list of suspects to work his way through. Plus, the hit man would still be walking around free, which would leave Billy's life in danger.

"I want to hang in here for at least a few more hours," he told Ken at last. "My gut's been saying that our guy's going to show up today. Of course, that was before I knew about Sherry Sherman."

"Yeah, well what are the odds he was watching her show?"

Probably not high, yet not zero, either. That was the trouble. However, there was no sense getting into a discussion about something they were both aware of, so he simply said, ''I'll check with the airlines. See how late I can leave here and still make it to New York before show time. There must be a red-eye I could catch.''

''Okay,'' Ken said. ''But hopefully you won't have to. With any luck, Billy will be in the next place I hit.''

''Right. If our killer *doesn't* show here, though, and you *don't* find Billy in the next little while...''

He rapidly thought through his plan one more time and concluded it had to be the best option.

''Well, I'll check in with you later,'' he said. ''See where we're at then. And good luck.''

''You too,'' Ken said before clicking off.

Dan put down his phone and scanned the wall of monitors again. At the exact instant he realized Mickey Westover was no longer standing in the yard, she said, ''Sounds as if you've got a problem.''

MICKEY MIGHT CONSIDER herself the queen of glaring contests, but the look Dan skewered her with when he wheeled around almost made her shiver.

''How long were you listening?'' he demanded.

''A couple of minutes,'' she said, setting her things on the counter so she could break eye contact without obviously backing down.

''I got chilly waiting outside,'' she added, even though there wasn't a chance he'd buy that. This was the middle of July and it was a hot day.

She didn't feel even a twinge of guilt, though. Not when he'd been lying to her since the moment he'd hit her with that tackle. And especially not when an awesome story had just fallen into her lap.

But she'd better be sure she had all the blanks filled in right.

"So somebody's out to kill Billy Brent," she said. "And you're expecting the guy to show up here."

"Forget you heard that."

"It's not an easy kind of thing to forget. Are we talking a hit man? A hired killer?"

When Dan didn't reply, she said, "Don't you know?"

Wow. She could actually see him getting madder. Obviously, he didn't like the implication that he was even marginally in the dark.

"It's probably a contract," he muttered at last.

Good, she was getting somewhere.

"And has this guy already tried to kill Billy? Or did someone warn him that there was a contract on him? I mean, how did he know he was in danger?"

Dan remained silent again, so she decided that asking him direct questions wasn't the way to go. She might be better off just hypothesizing.

"I gather Billy's been in hiding," she pressed on. "But now he's gone to New York. And if the killer's heard about that TV appearance, he—"

"Look," Dan snapped. "First, this is none of your business. Second, I don't intend to discuss it with you. And third, just keep it entirely to yourself."

She stared at him for a moment, wondering whether he actually thought there was even a remote chance of that.

For a journalist, a scoop like this one was heaven-sent. And she was the only journalist who had even an inkling about it, which made it that much better.

''Obviously,'' Dan added, ''Billy is thousands of miles away, and that means you're not going to get your interview. So since I *am* expecting the killer to show up, the sooner you get out of here the better. Where's your car?''

''Down the road.''

''Fine. I'll drive you to it. Let's get going.''

''Uh-uh. I'm staying.''

''What?''

His expression said he didn't believe he could have heard right, so she said, ''Look, whether the killer comes here or you go to New York to help your friend find Billy, this is a major story. And I want it.''

''What?'' he said a second time, giving her an even more incredulous look.

''I said I want the story. Don't you think I have aspirations beyond Arts and Entertainment?''

''How the hell should I know? We've barely met.''

''Well, I do. I want to see my byline on the front page every now and then. Preferably, *more* than every now and then. Dan, this is the kind of story that will do a lot to make that happen, and I might never get as good a chance again. So however things play out, I want an exclusive for the *Post*.''

''Listen to me carefully,'' he said, enunciating his

words clearly. "There is no story. There are only the two of us heading to your car. Period."

Telling herself it was time for another change of tactics, she shrugged and reached for her laptop.

"Okay. If that's the way it is, then I'll have to simply write up what I have and e-mail it to my editor. It won't be nearly the scoop I was hoping for, but just the fact that somebody's trying to kill Billy Brent will sell a lot of papers."

"Fine. If selling papers is so important to you, go right ahead and put Billy's life at even greater risk than it already is."

"How would I be doing that? If somebody's already trying to kill him, how would my reporting it put him at any more risk? In fact, it could do the opposite. The publicity might make the killer back off."

Dan was clearly annoyed by her logic, but he didn't try to argue with it.

Not arguing, though, was a long way from cooperating. And without his help she wasn't going to get the whole story, which she desperately wanted.

"Do whatever you like," he muttered at last. "It doesn't really matter, because by tomorrow's edition this will be over. Either the killer will have shown up here, in which case I'll have taken care of him, or we'll have Billy back in hiding."

"Tomorrow's edition?" she said in her best puzzled manner.

"Well, you're too late for today's—unless the *Post* comes out hours after most papers."

"But I wasn't talking about the print edition. This is what we call breaking news. If I give the story to my boss it'll be the lead in our online edition within minutes. So...well, maybe you'd like to reconsider. Because if you promise me an exclusive of the entire thing, I'll hold back now."

"You're trying to blackmail me," he snapped.

"No. I'm only negotiating a deal."

"I HAVE TO KNOW whether I can trust her," Dan said into his cell phone.

As Lydia said "No problem," he glanced at the library door.

He'd closed it tightly before making his call, because he already knew there was at least one thing about Mickey Westover that he *couldn't* trust. She had no compunction when it came to eavesdropping.

However, he was speaking quietly and that was a solid-core door.

"So check out her reputation in general," he continued. "And specifically contact some of the other celebrities she's done these articles on. See if anything appeared in print that she assured them wouldn't."

"No problem," Lydia said again, her tone amused this time—letting him know that she didn't need him telling her how to do her job.

And she didn't, of course. All of the research operatives at Risk Control International were good, but she was the best.

"I need to hear back soon," he added, although he probably didn't have to tell her that, either.

"You've got it, Dan. I'll call and let you know whatever I can learn fast. Then, if it's necessary, I'll start digging more thoroughly."

"Good. Thanks, Lydia."

"That's what I'm here for."

Dan clicked off and started back to where he'd left Mickey in the kitchen.

He was feeling marginally better, but only marginally.

Oh, hell, who was he trying to kid? He was still fit to be tied.

As clichéd as that phrase might be, it was the best one he could think of to describe how he was feeling—although *downright homicidal* was certainly a strong contender.

He didn't recall ever having seriously considered murdering someone before, not even any of the low-life he'd dealt with during his years as a cop. But right this minute he could cheerfully strangle Mickey Westover.

She *was* trying to blackmail him into agreeing to what she wanted—regardless of how she put it. And as much as he disliked the idea of agreeing to a damn thing…

Ken Heath had been right. The odds were low that whoever was stalking Billy had caught this morning's Sherry Sherman Show.

However, if news about a hit man being after Billy

went online it would immediately be picked up by every TV and radio station in North America.

And it was far too easy to picture Billy's would-be killer driving through the mountains, almost here, when the car radio told him that he was heading straight into a trap—because Mickey had included that information in her story.

Yes, *downright homicidal* was definitely right up there with *fit to be tied.*

Eyeing Mickey's slender throat, he imagined his hands wrapped around it.

All that did, though, was start him thinking that if her pale skin felt as smooth as it looked, then once he'd touched it, strangling her would be the last thing on his mind.

He told himself to lose that thought.

Mickey Westover might be a good-looking woman, and he'd admit there was something awfully sexy about her, but she was annoying as hell.

Of course, she was just trying to get ahead, which wasn't something he'd fault her for under different circumstances.

And now that he'd had time to consider, he realized that she didn't really represent a serious problem. Not short-term, at least.

At the moment, all he had to do was prevent her from calling her boss back. Or using her computer to e-mail him.

But sending her packing wasn't the way to handle things. Even if he confiscated her laptop and cell phone before showing her the door, she'd find a pay phone.

So he'd have to negotiate, to use her term. He only intended to negotiate a little, though.

CHAPTER THREE

ONCE DAN GOT BACK to the kitchen, Mickey eyed him expectantly.

''Okay,'' he said. ''Here's the deal I'll go for. If the killer shows up, you get your exclusive this afternoon. If he doesn't, if I have to go to New York and find Billy, you don't breathe a word about any of this until the situation is resolved. *Then,* you get your exclusive.''

She looked suspicious, so he added, ''Either way, you win.''

''And what if you end up in New York and another journalist gets wind of what's happening?'' she said. ''Where would my exclusive be then?''

''Don't worry about that, because this will be over and done with today. Now, give me your laptop and purse.''

''Pardon me?''

''Your laptop and purse,'' he repeated. ''Just for a minute.''

She hesitated, then handed them over.

''Oh, and one other thing,'' he said.

''What?''

''When you get down to writing your story, you

can report the facts of what happens. And Billy's a public figure so he's fair game. But my name doesn't show up in print."

"Then how do I refer to you?"

"Mr. Brent's bodyguard will do. And there can't be any mention of the company I work for, either."

"You mean you don't work for Billy?"

"Only indirectly. At any rate, those are the other ground rules. And before we go any further, I want your word that you won't break them."

She nodded, although she clearly didn't like having additional parameters. But since there was a lot about this *he* didn't like, it only seemed fair.

"Oh, and I should tell you," he continued, "that a lot of important people deal with my company. People who like the fact that it's low profile.

"So if you did happen to make any mention of me—or it—you'd be done at the *Post.* And you'd never get a job with a decent paper again."

"Are you threatening me?"

"No. I'm only negotiating a deal."

When he began rummaging through her purse, she said, "What do you figure you're doing?"

"Just taking your car keys and phone."

"I don't think so!"

Sticking the keys into his pocket, he tossed her purse back, then started across the kitchen with her phone and computer.

"Give me my other things," she demanded.

Ignoring her was immensely enjoyable.

After dumping the newspapers out of the recycle

box, he took a minute to check the surveillance monitors.

They still weren't picking up anything unusual. And even though he hated the idea of leaving them unmanned again, he hated the thought of Mickey getting in touch with the *Post* even more. Which meant that the best thing he could do was just get this over with as quickly as possible.

He put her laptop, cell phone and keys into the box, then picked it up and began making his way from room to room with it—her on his heels—unplugging each phone he came to and adding it to the box.

"I don't believe this," she finally muttered. "I simply do not believe you're doing this."

"You told me you wanted to stay," he reminded her. "So you don't need your car keys right now. And you haven't got the story yet, so you don't need your computer."

"Well I certainly need a phone. I promised my boss I'd call him back."

"He'll understand. In the long run."

Apparently, she couldn't think of a response to that. She followed him silently into the last room, a huge, windowless theater that could seat twenty.

He unplugged the phone in there and topped up the pile with it, then said, "Okay. You stay here. If you hear any shots, hit the floor between the rows of chairs."

"And how am I supposed to get my story from in here?"

"If the killer shows up, I'll knock him unconscious and then fill you in. You can even take pictures."

"But—"

"Mickey, the odds are very high that we're talking about a professional hit man. Just letting you stay goes against my better judgement, and I definitely don't have time to baby-sit."

"I don't need baby-sitting. I even know how to handle a gun. I used to take target shooting with my brothers."

"You don't have a gun, though, do you? So just sit tight."

"But—"

"That's how it has to be," he snapped. "Take it or leave it."

"All right," she said sullenly.

He walked out of the room—closing the door behind himself, despite knowing damn well that she'd have it cracked open within thirty seconds—and headed back to the kitchen once more.

The monitors were still showing nothing out of the ordinary, so unless his killer had snuck up tight to the house during the past five minutes...

That thought didn't sit well with him. Considering the way the day had been going so far, it just might have happened.

After concealing the recycle box in the back of a closet, keeping only his own cell phone accessible, he scanned the screens again.

The unsettled feeling worming its way around in

his stomach was telling him that he'd better make sure things were still cool, so he took his Glock from his waistband and headed for the front door.

If he discovered someone plastered against the outside of the house, the way he'd found Mickey earlier, at least he'd have the element of surprise.

He silently unbolted the door and threw it open—his gun ready for action.

But there was no new company. Not out front, anyway.

Still, he'd better take a quick walk around the house. Be certain that he hadn't missed seeing anything.

He strode down from the porch and started off, pausing to listen for a moment when he reached the corner.

All he heard was the raucous call of a jay and the clicking sound that some insect made when it flew.

So far so good. Then he headed around the corner and found himself face-to-face with big trouble.

Actually, face to mask, he thought uneasily.

A man wearing a rubber mask that made him look like an alien was standing five feet in front of him—with a Magnum centered on his chest.

"Put down your gun," the masked man said. "Slowly."

Wordlessly Dan set his Glock on the ground.

"Good. Now we're going into the house. You first."

He turned and began walking back toward the front door, both his heart and his thoughts racing.

Most likely, he was only still breathing because this guy figured Billy was inside and hadn't wanted to alert him with a shot.

But he couldn't count on staying alive for long. Not when professional killers tended to have a take-no-prisoners, leave-no-witnesses style of thinking.

However, the man didn't know the house and Dan did. Which meant that all he needed was one little break.

Adrenaline pumping, he stepped inside.

"Where's Billy?" the killer asked.

"This way."

He started across the polished pine floor of the entrance area, wishing he had eyes in the back of his head.

Ages ago, he'd perfected a move that would work if the man was close enough. At least, it had worked a few times in the past, in dark New Orleans alleys.

But if he guessed wrong and the killer was too far back, he'd get himself shot for sure. Then this guy would search the place and Mickey would take the next round of bullets.

So he couldn't guess. He'd just have to hope to hell that—

"Stop dead and put your hands up," Mickey ordered.

There was his break!

He whirled around and dove toward the floor in one motion, catching the killer around the knees as the Magnum exploded.

They both went sprawling and the gun skittered across the floor, vanishing beneath a massive desk.

The killer swore, grabbing Dan by the throat.

He slammed his fist into the guy's face hard enough to make him let go. Then there was another deafening shot. Just as he realized that Mickey must have fired again, she screamed, "Stop! Both of you!"

Instinctively he glanced in her direction, which proved to be a really stupid move. The killer caught him with such a wicked fist to the temple that it almost knocked him senseless.

While bells were bonging inside his head, the other man tore out of the place.

Mickey slammed the door shut after him, threw the bolt, then hurried over to where Dan was sitting on the floor.

She had a semiautomatic in one hand. The other, she tentatively rested on his shoulder, saying, "Are you okay?"

"I've got to catch him," he told her, managing to lurch to his feet.

"Dan, I don't think—"

"There's only one way he can go. And I can drive that road faster than someone who doesn't know it."

He reached for her gun; she whipped it behind her back and said, "Let's give that idea some thought."

DAN FELT AS IF he'd been hit with a tire iron rather than a fist, and when he tried to ask Mickey where she'd gotten a gun no words came out, which he took to be a bad sign.

If not for that, and if he had more confidence about getting farther than the porch without collapsing, he'd wrestle Mickey for the gun and head after the killer.

Given the reality of the situation, however, he simply stood waiting to hear what she'd say next.

"Dan, you hardly look up to chasing after a hit man," she began. "And for all we know, he has another gun in his car or wherever."

Right. And he'd need another one. That Magnum was still lying under the desk.

Everything had happened so quickly that Dan had almost forgotten about it. But he'd dig it out before he left. It never hurt to have an extra weapon.

"So if he does have a second gun," Mickey was saying, "and you go looking for him, you might end up awfully sorry."

He'd have nodded that she had a point, only he suspected the movement would make his head explode.

"I should have shot him," she said more quietly. "Instead of simply firing into the air, I should have shot him in the leg or something. I was afraid of hitting you, though. Then he sprinted by me like a track star and that was that."

"It's okay," he managed to say. "You probably kept us both from getting killed. So…thanks."

When she smiled and said he was welcome, the

thought that she had a great smile somehow found its way into his mind.

He wasn't sure which was more bizarre—the fact that he was having the thought at all or that he was having it while his head was pounding.

At any rate, he told it to find its way back out, then put together the words to ask where the gun had come from.

"It was in a drawer," she told him. "In the theater. I don't usually go poking around in other people's drawers," she continued quickly. "But you seemed certain the killer was going to show up, and I remembered reading somewhere that Billy kept guns around."

"Ah," he said. Then he gingerly touched his temple to see whether it had started to swell.

Not surprisingly, it had.

"We should put ice on that," Mickey said.

Before he could tell her he didn't have time to waste on first aid, she added, "Why don't you go sit down and I'll get some."

Sitting down struck him as an excellent suggestion. But since his cell was lying on the kitchen counter, and he didn't trust her not to grab it and call her editor, he followed along to make sure she wouldn't, his head only hurting a little more with each step he took.

He picked up the phone and clipped it to his belt, thinking that even though his plan to lure the killer here had worked, the end result sure wasn't what he'd been hoping for.

So now he was back to square one, and there wasn't a chance in the world of that guy giving up. He'd try something again, just as soon as he had a good opportunity—which, unless Ken lucked out in New York, could well be tomorrow morning.

"Here," Mickey said, handing him some ice wrapped in a dish towel.

"Thanks." He pressed the ice pack to his temple, saying, "I've got to make a call."

That was her cue to give him privacy, of course, but when she pretended not to pick up on the hint, he couldn't be bothered making a big deal out of it.

Since she already knew the basic story, what would it matter if she listened in on the next installment?

He got hold of Ken and asked whether he'd found Billy yet.

"Still working on it," he said. "But I have to admit I'm losing hope. Anything happen there?"

"Yeah, and it wasn't pretty."

He began filling the other man in, trying not to think that Ken must figure he was an idiot.

What else would he think, though?

It was just a good thing he was the type to keep quiet. Because Dan O'Neill setting a trap for a killer, and then entirely missing the guy's arrival, was so much *not* the norm for him that a lot of people would find it too damn funny.

After he finished relating the basics of what had happened, Ken said, "Are you still hearing bells?"

"No, I'm fine now."

And that was only a slight exaggeration. He *was* feeling a lot better than he'd been a few minutes ago.

"But Billy sure isn't going to be fine," he added. "Not if this guy gets to him before we do."

"And we don't have any more idea of who we're up against than we did before," Ken said.

"Uh-uh. His mask was the kind that pulls down over the head. So all I know is that he's average height, average build, and hits like a heavyweight."

"You think he's going to hear about Billy being on Sherry Sherman's show?"

"Yeah, I think there's a real good chance. Even if he's still thinking Billy's holed up here, he wouldn't come back. He'll realize that his first visit put me on high alert, which would make a second one too dangerous. So now he'll start planning a different approach. And he'll hear about the show as soon as he begins nosing around for fresh information."

"I assume you'll be leaving for New York right away, then."

"As soon as I can get a flight. I didn't have a chance to check on them, but I'll just head to the airport and take whatever's available."

"Well, I'll keep looking here."

"Right. And I'll call you again later."

"So," Mickey said as he clipped the phone to his belt once more. "We're on our way to New York now."

We? He almost laughed.

Did she figure that getting punched in the head

had given him amnesia? That she'd be able to convince him he'd agreed to more than he had?

If so, she was about to be very disappointed.

"*I'm* going to New York," he told her. "Alone."

"But—"

"No," he said firmly. "Our deal wasn't that you'd go along. It was that, if I went, you'd stay here and get your exclusive once the excitement was over. And that you wouldn't breathe a word about the story until then."

"But things have changed."

"Meaning?"

She shrugged. "Meaning I kept you from getting killed. I *probably* did," she added before he had the chance to correct her.

"Plus, that ice is working wonders. I can hardly see any swelling now. So all in all, you owe me."

Ah. She was trying emotional blackmail this time around.

"Maybe I do," he admitted. "But I don't owe you a trip to New York."

He set down the ice pack and picked up the semiautomatic she'd put on the counter, then started toward the front door.

"Wait a minute," she said.

He kept walking, not even remotely surprised when she followed him.

"Look," he said, stopping a few feet short of the door. "This isn't open for discussion. My gun's outside and I'm going to get it. After that, I intend to throw a few things into a suitcase and—"

"So you're expecting to be in New York for a while?"

"No, I doubt I'll be there long. But the only way I can get a gun on a plane is in checked luggage."

"People can still do that? Doesn't airport security X-ray everything these days? Whether it's checked or not?"

"Uh-huh. But my stuff gets special treatment."

"What?" she said, looking as if she figured he was delusional.

He simply shrugged. He didn't care whether she thought he was crazy, and he had no intention of getting into any hows and whys with her—although the "arrangement" his company had for transporting guns was really a blessing.

It wasn't always easy to acquire the sort of weapon you wanted when you'd just arrived in a city.

"You mean," she was saying, "that you can walk into any airport, carrying anything you like in your luggage and—"

"I didn't say *anything I like.* I said guns. Now let's drop it, okay?" he added as he took a few final steps to the door.

Cautiously he opened it and surveyed the clearing, virtually certain the killer wouldn't have hung around but not wanting to take any chances.

Then he glanced at her again, and said, "Would you mind waiting inside?"

For once, she did as he asked and simply stood in the doorway while he collected his Glock.

As he headed back up the porch steps, she said, "I could be a big help in New York."

"I told you it wasn't open for discussion," he reminded her.

"Then we won't discuss," she said, trailing after him when he started toward his room. "I'll talk and you just listen."

TURK HAD RUN like hell almost the entire way from Billy Brent's place back to where he'd left his rental car—hidden down an old pull-off that was so overgrown it couldn't have been used in years. For a city slicker, he'd done well to even spot it.

He climbed into the driver's seat and took his Beretta from the glove compartment in case things went even further off course.

Then he powered down the windows, thinking that he hadn't had such a close call in...hell, he'd probably *never* had such a close one. But at least he knew where the problem lay. It was simply that he was out of his element.

Maybe contract killers *did* have to go wherever their work took them, but Vancouver Island was so different from Manhattan it could be on another planet.

He was used to bright lights and big city noise. So put him in the wilderness and it was hardly surprising that he wasn't totally on top of his game.

Oh, not that the entire island was wall-to-wall forest. He'd landed in a city. Actually, to be specific, he'd landed in its harbor. But same difference.

Victoria. The capital of British Columbia, a fact he'd carefully tucked away.

He was a trivia nut, and after millions of hours of *Jeopardy* and *Wheel* and *Millionaire* he could usually come up with at least some inconsequential fact relating to just about any subject.

Foreign geography, however, was his weak suit. So whenever he traveled he paid special attention to names and places.

At any rate, from what little he'd seen of Victoria it seemed like a nice place. And only half an hour by float plane north of Seattle.

Still, once you left the city behind, there was nothing except mile after mile of mountains and trees, and he just didn't get the appeal of this nature crap. You wanted nature, you went to Central Park. You didn't head for Canada and total isolation.

He didn't, anyway. Not unless someone was paying him big bucks to make the trip, which, of course, explained why he was here.

But when it came to Billy Brent, the guy made over twenty million a picture. He could afford to be anywhere in the world on his downtime. So why would he want to spend a single day of it in the middle of nowhere?

Oh, hell, he was back to thinking about Billy Brent and his damned retreat. And what a screwup that scene had been.

It would have been even worse, though, if he wasn't in good shape. All those hours at the gym—

in the ring, lifting weights, running laps—had really paid off today.

If he hadn't landed that one smoker of a punch he might be in real trouble now. Because whoever the guy at Billy's was, he wasn't any pushover. That one punch had probably made the difference between getting away and not.

Of course, the important thing was that he *had* gotten away.

But that bitch with the gun had surprised the shit out of him and if he ever laid eyes on her again she'd be dead.

Hell, she'd be dead already if his Magnum hadn't gone flying, which was another point against her. Her sneaking up on him had cost him his favorite piece.

That had him royally pissed, and it wasn't the only thing that was frosting him off.

This job should already be over and done with. But because of her, it wasn't.

He thought about that for a minute, then backed up his logic a little.

If not for her, the job would be over and done with, assuming that Billy Brent had actually been in there. Which might not have been the case.

What if Billy had realized he was being targeted?

That could be. And it would mean all the media crap about his being at his retreat had been nothing but a setup.

Turk lit a cigarette and filled his lungs with the hot smoke, feeling pretty much back to normal now, able to contemplate where things stood with a clear brain.

He'd pegged the guy with the Glock for a bodyguard. Maybe that wasn't it, though. Maybe he'd been there instead of Billy, waiting to see whether anyone came looking for the superstar.

But if Billy wasn't there, where was he?

After considering the question, he retrieved his laptop from the floor of the back seat, thinking he'd better see—courtesy of the world of wireless Internet connections—if there was anything new going on in Billy's life.

Once he was into cyberspace, he clicked on his bookmark for the best of the Billy Brent fan sites he'd found.

The message scrolling across the top of the screen read, ''Watch Billy tomorrow morning! Live on the Sherry Sherman Show!''

Well. Wasn't that interesting.

He read the text saying that Sherry had announced Billy would be her special guest. Then he got off the Internet and shut the laptop, smiling to himself.

He'd really grown to love modern technology.

CHAPTER FOUR

WHILE MICKEY DID HER BEST to convince Dan that taking her to New York with him was a first-rate idea, he tossed enough clothes into a suitcase to keep the killer's gun and his own, from rattling around.

Not that he was about to pack his Glock just yet. He wanted it loaded and accessible until he had a flight lined up and was ready to check in.

Life had handed him enough surprises that he always felt more comfortable when he was carrying.

"...so I'd get the breaking story firsthand, which would save both of us time," Mickey was saying. "And you and this Ken fellow would have my help.

"I *can* use a gun," she elaborated. "I mean, for more than shooting into the air to get someone's attention."

Man, oh, man. Just what they'd need. An intrepid girl reporter with a gun.

"When all's said and done," she added, "it comes down to a totally win-win arrangement."

She finally stopped speaking and eyed him expectantly.

He rubbed his jaw as if considering a positive response.

Needless to say, he really wasn't. She was definitely not going along.

Despite the case she'd made, she'd likely get in the way.

Even if she didn't, this was strictly a job for professionals and she was a civilian, which meant that if he let her go with him he'd feel responsible for her safety. And that was something he didn't need.

Besides, the jury was still out on whether he could trust her.

Glancing at his watch, he wondered how soon he'd hear back from Lydia. But regardless of what she unearthed about Mickey, it really rankled him that the woman was trying to revise their deal in her favor—especially when this assignment would already be wrapped up if not for her.

If she hadn't come back after he'd sent her away, he'd have been watching the monitors when the killer arrived.

By now, the guy would either be dead or in police custody. So Mickey could claim he owed her all she wanted, but he wasn't buying into any guilt trip.

Regardless of that, though, he'd rather not tell her she wasn't going to New York simply because he didn't want her along. Not after she'd been gutsy enough to confront their hit man.

It would be kinder to convince her that it just wasn't a good idea.

Kinder.

He seldom concerned himself about being kind. But these circumstances were more than a little unusual. He couldn't remember the last time he'd needed help because someone was holding a gun on him.

So when she finally became tired of waiting for him to speak up, and gave him an impatient "Well?" he did his best to sound eminently reasonable.

"Look," he said. "I know how badly you want to be there when this wraps up, but your going with me simply isn't a good plan."

"Why not?"

He shrugged. "Just for starters, if *my* wife or girlfriend or whatever announced that she was waltzing off to the far side of the continent with a strange man—"

"You don't have a wife or girlfriend or whatever," she interrupted.

He had no idea how she knew that, but before he could ask she was saying, "And I don't have a husband or a whatever, so that argument's irrelevant."

"What about your job, then? What would your boss say?"

"I want to go *because* of my job," she said, eyeing him as if he was a simpleton. "To get the story."

"What I mean is that the Billy Brent interview can't be the only assignment you're working on."

"Well, no, but—"

"And where would the money come from? Do you have any idea how much last-minute tickets cost?"

"Of course. I don't live in a cave."

"Okay, then you know you're talking a small fortune for the flight alone. And aside from everything else, surely the *Post* wouldn't send an Arts and Entertainment journalist to cover the sort of story we have here. I mean, a hit man with a contract on Billy Brent has to be such big news it—''

''I'll make you another deal,'' she interrupted.

He reminded himself that he wasn't buying into any guilt trip.

Then she quietly said, ''Dan, you can't imagine how important this is for my career.''

''Yes, I can.''

And, hell, maybe it *was* important. But he had his own career to consider. And he sure didn't want any more potential complications.

But the next thing he knew, he was saying, ''Exactly what have you got in mind?''

She looked very relieved; it didn't make him the least bit happier that he'd opened his mouth.

''If I can convince my editor to okay the assignment *and* authorize my expenses,'' she said, ''you'll stop objecting and take me along.''

Her words made him feel better. She couldn't seriously expect her boss to not only give her the time but the money as well. Could she?

He really doubted it. Hard news stories went to hard news reporters. Period.

''So?'' she said.

His phone began to ring, temporarily saving him from her question.

''Dan O'Neill,'' he answered.

''Dan, it's Lydia.''

''Hi,'' he said, turning away from Mickey even though he knew that wouldn't keep her from hearing.

''I've talked to several people about Mickey Westover, and it doesn't sound as if you have anything to worry about. She has a reputation for being a straight shooter.''

''And things that are said…''

''In confidence?'' Lydia supplied, probably guessing that Mickey was right there.

''Uh-huh.''

''All my sources assured me there'd been no problems.''

''Good. That's good to know. Anything else?''

''Nothing negative. I'm going to keep at this. There are a few more avenues I want to explore. But I'm not really expecting to turn up anything problematic.''

''Good,'' he said again. ''If you do, though…''

''You'll know almost as soon as I do.''

''Fine. And thanks.''

He clicked off, telling himself he couldn't have asked for better news.

Lydia might have said she was going to keep checking, but she never gave a positive preliminary report unless she was damned sure she wouldn't get any surprises later on.

Even so, the fact that he didn't have to worry about Mickey double-crossing him wasn't going to make him change his mind. He and Ken would be far better off without her.

"Where were we?" he said, turning back toward her.

"Just about to make a deal."

"I don't think we were quite to that point."

She gazed at him for a moment, as if trying to figure out exactly what he was thinking, then said, "Dan, I know I'm repeating myself, but I just don't believe you can *really* realize how much this would mean to me. And all I'm asking for is the chance to convince my boss."

He hesitated, knowing he'd feel better if she thought that he was at least giving her a chance. And surely she'd never persuade the guy to go along with her.

"Okay, have a shot at it," he said, assuring himself he was looking at virtually no risk.

She held out her hand for his cell phone, which reminded him that the rest of the phones—including hers—were still sitting in that recycle box.

He turned his cellular over to her, then nonchalantly zipped his suitcase shut.

Her conversation shouldn't take more than about thirty seconds. And once her boss had said "No dice," all there'd be left to do was drop her off at her car. After that, he'd be done with her.

THE MORE MICKEY TALKED, the less Dan liked what he was hearing.

Somehow or other, she'd succeeded in presenting her absurd idea in such a logical-sounding way that it no longer seemed half as absurd.

When she lapsed into silence, obviously listening to whatever her boss was saying, he desperately wished he could hear both sides of the conversation.

Her expression made him certain that this Eric fellow was not telling her there was absolutely no way. Which was what was supposed to be happening.

Dammit. He felt like kicking himself for not realizing how convincing she could be. Because he sure as hell should have.

After all, at this point she'd convinced him to agree to two of her ridiculous deals.

"I know, Eric," she said. "You're perfectly right. I'm not the best candidate. I'm not claiming to be.

"But the critical thing is that I'm the one up here with Dan O'Neill and he trusts me."

Oh, right. *Trust* was a definite stretch.

Maybe he believed that Mickey wouldn't renege on her word. After all, Lydia just didn't get things like that wrong. But that didn't mean he entirely trusted the woman.

She was a schemer, a sneak, a blackmailer, a—

"And since I'm the only person he's willing to take along..." she was saying.

Willing to take along? That was hardly the way he'd put it.

"Yes, I *am* positive about that. He just doesn't have much faith in most journalists."

Finally. Something that was true.

"But the two of us clicked, and...well, he isn't giving us any real choice."

When she paused, he found himself holding his breath, waiting for her clincher.

"Either you assign *me* to the story," she concluded, "or we don't get it."

There was a small silence before she said, "Yes, I really do think I'm up to it. And the prospect of letting it slip through our fingers...we're talking a hit man trying to kill Billy Brent. We're talking not only that, which none of our competition even knows about, but exclusive coverage of what happens from here on in.

"Eric, it'll be a huge story. And only the *Post* will have it. We'll scoop both the *Chronicle* and the *Examiner*. Hell, we'll scoop *The New York Times!*"

Dan could feel his anxiety level rising. Mickey Westover was making him very nervous.

She glanced over and gave him a warm smile. It sent a chill down his spine. The fact she felt like smiling wasn't good.

The silence stretched until he couldn't keep himself from whispering, "Is he going for it?"

"Going, going, gone," she said. "I'm on hold and he's on his other line, running the idea past the editor in chief for an okay."

Oh, man. But surely an editor in chief would recognize the insanity of this.

He began willing that to happen.

And then Mickey said, "Eric, that's great. Please thank Mr. Edwards for me. And I promise I'll come through, that neither of you will be disappointed."

THE ONLY AVAILABLE SEATS had been in first class, and since Mickey had never flown anything but economy before that had simply added to her excitement, so much so that she was barely worrying about whether Eric would drop dead from shock when he saw her expense report.

Or about the fact that paying for her ticket had probably put her within two dollars of maxing out her Visa card. Which meant that the car rental people were in for an unpleasant surprise.

Dan had said there was no time to waste returning the Taurus, so they'd driven down to Victoria in his four-by-four and left the car at Billy's to be picked up. But once it had been retrieved, and someone tried to get authorization for what she owed them…

Well, her MasterCard wasn't at its limit, so as soon as she had a chance she'd phone and give them that number. Otherwise, her credit rating would be in the tank.

As the plane lifted off, she took another slow, deep breath. It was only for insurance, though. She already felt pretty much back to normal.

There was barely any queasiness left in her stomach, and her intuition was saying that everything would be fine from here on in. Travelwise, at least.

Thus far, however, it had been a banner day in that department.

Of course, things had been even more exciting in the hit man department. But that was something she'd be wiser not to think about. Remembering how hard she'd been shaking, while pointing that gun at the killer, was a lot tougher on her nerves than focusing her thoughts on her travel adventures.

Adventures. She paused on the word, then decided it was the right one.

Driving with Dan, while he'd taken those tight mountain curves at roughly eight hundred miles an hour, had definitely been an adventure. And there wasn't the slightest doubt that the flight from Victoria to Seattle qualified.

It had been her first time in a seaplane, and she'd quite happily go through the rest of her life without a second one. Their descent had been steep enough to convince her that the pilot was suicidal and intending to drown everyone aboard.

But now that she and Dan were on a nice, safe 757, en route to New York, it would be smooth sailing. Or smooth flying, to be precise.

"Would you like something to drink?" a flight attendant asked.

Dan opted for a beer.

Since the woman was holding an open bottle of champagne, Mickey chose that.

She took a sip, pleased to discover that her stomach was going to handle the bubbles just fine. Then she began wishing that Dan seemed happier about having her along.

Well, more accurately, she wished he didn't seem downright miserable. And that he liked her. Even a bit.

Things would be far more comfortable if the air

between them wasn't heavy with negative vibes, not a single one of which was coming from her.

After all, how could she possibly feel unkindly toward a man who was letting her in on the scoop of a lifetime? Even if he had done a lot of foot-dragging before agreeing. And aside from helping her get a major career break, he was really sort of cute.

She considered that for a few seconds, aware of how drastically her opinion of his attractiveness had changed since they'd met. Obviously, he was the type of man who grew on people.

Oh, she still wasn't crazy about his short hair, but that type of thing was easy to fix. And she was sure the coldness in his blue eyes would dissipate if he just began warming up to her.

And that little scar above his upper lip...she'd been wondering exactly how he'd come by it.

Actually, she'd been wondering a lot of things about him. And since most men loved talking about themselves, what better way of warming him up than getting him to do exactly that?

"So," she said.

He glanced at her.

She shot him a friendly smile and tried not to feel badly when he didn't return it.

After a few beats, she said, "I haven't forgotten what you were saying earlier—that you don't want your name in print. Or any mention of the company you work for. But is it okay if I ask you about it? Completely off the record?"

''Ask me what about it?''

''Well, for starters, it must have a name.''

''You wouldn't recognize it.''

''I might.''

Dan broke eye contact with Mickey and sat gazing out the window for a moment, considering where he should go from here.

Given what Lydia had learned, he figured he could believe Mickey when she said ''off the record.'' So it wouldn't hurt to tell her a bit about RCI.

Besides, even though the company kept a low profile its existence was hardly a state secret. And Mickey was a journalist.

She'd know exactly where to look for whatever information she was interested in finding, which meant that it would probably take her all of five minutes to learn most of what she might want to about either RCI or him.

Confidential information had almost become a thing of the past.

He drank some of his beer, then said, ''The company's called Risk Control International.''

''Oh. Okay, you were right. I've never heard of it.''

''Most people haven't. It's in the survival business.''

''You mean wilderness survival?''

''No. I mean keeping people alive.''

''Oh,'' she said again.

For a moment he thought she was done, but then she said, ''So it provides bodyguards?''

"Uh-huh. That's one thing. It also runs a lot of training courses. Most of them are basically aimed at law enforcement types, but they attract civilian students, too—usually executives who work in countries with terrorism problems, or other people at high risk."

"And the courses teach...?"

Man, the way she could fire questions made him suspect she was a better reporter than he'd been giving her credit for.

"They cover things like self-defense, tactical driving, handgun training," he told her. "And there's one called Special Technics that touches on everything from hot-wiring cars to picking locks."

"People need to know those sorts of things to stay alive?"

"Sometimes. You can never tell what kind of jam you'll find yourself in. At any rate, the company can pretty well provide any service, handle anything a client needs. Most people working for it are independent contractors, which gives it a large pool of experts to draw on."

"Is that what you are, then? An independent contractor? And an expert?"

"Uh-huh. I'm a personal security advisor, which basically means that I analyze a situation, settle on a way of safeguarding the individual—or individuals—at risk, and then take things from there."

"And that was what you did in Billy's case."

"Right. Only the plan should have gone a whole lot more smoothly. All it involved was Billy laying low with Ken Heath, who also does work for RCI, while I lured the killer to the retreat. Then, according to the script, once he got there I'd make him tell me who'd hired him. After that, I'd turn both him and the information over to the police.''

''*Make* him tell you?''

He merely shrugged. He wasn't getting into that with her.

For a moment she looked as if she was going to try pressing him about it, but she finally just said, ''Do you have any idea who *might* have hired this guy? I mean, I'm assuming you discussed that with Billy.''

''Of course.''

''And he thought it could be...?''

''The list is endless. I'm exaggerating,'' he added quickly, even though he wasn't exaggerating by a lot.

''In any event,'' he continued, deciding it would be wise to change the conversation's direction, ''what happened today just goes to show how even the most straightforward plan can fall apart.

''Billy wasn't supposed to give Ken the slip and head for New York, I wasn't supposed to end up on the wrong end of a gun and the killer wasn't supposed to get away.''

He had another swig of beer, assuming he must have satisfied her curiosity by now.

However, she barely waited for him to swallow before saying, ''But now that he did get away, and now that you think he might show up at NBS in the morning, how will you deal with it?''

"Well, if we haven't found Billy before then, we'll go with Plan B—watching to see if the hit man *does* show up at NBS. And insuring Billy's safety if that happens."

Mickey looked thoughtful, then said, "I asked you about this before, but you didn't tell me. How did Billy know someone was trying to kill him?"

When he hesitated, she added, "I wouldn't use it in a story unless I'd checked with him, first."

"Yeah, okay," he said slowly, reminding himself once more that he didn't have much reason to be overly cautious. He'd never known Lydia to make a mistake.

Besides, as soon as Billy was back in circulation he'd be telling anyone and everyone what had happened. He knew their star well enough to be sure of that.

Focusing on Mickey again, he said, "A couple of weeks ago, Billy almost totaled his Porsche—was incredibly lucky that he only got shaken up. And when his mechanic checked over what was left of the car, he discovered that the brakes had been tampered with.

"Then he had a look at Billy's other vehicles and found that someone had done the same thing with all six of them. That was when his people contacted RCI."

"And RCI contacted you."

"Uh-huh."

He watched her take a sip of champagne, absently thinking that he'd never in a million years have imagined today unfolding as it had, would never have pictured himself winging his way across the country at all, let alone with a beautiful woman who smelled like…

It took a minute, then it came to him. Her scent reminded him of New Orleans. Made him think about jasmine and four-o'clocks, about the Garden District on a lazy summer evening.

What on earth was he doing, though? Why in hell was he thinking about her scent when she was only sitting here with him because she'd blackmailed him into bringing her along?

His anger came drifting back and settled around him like a dark cloud. He'd never liked manipulative women, and he certainly wasn't going to make an exception when it came to this one. So he'd be wise to stop even looking at her, let alone thinking how great she smelled.

"It must be exciting work," she said. "Constantly getting people out of trouble. But what kind of background does a person need to become a personal security advisor?"

Something in his expression must have told her he was getting tired of her reporter approach, because she quickly added, "I'm sorry. Asking questions is my job and I know I sometimes do too much of it. It's an occupational hazard."

She seemed so contrite that he merely shrugged again.

He didn't normally talk much about himself, but

it wouldn't really hurt to do a little more of it at the moment.

This was a long flight, and sitting in silence would only make it seem longer.

CHAPTER FIVE

MICKEY HAD PRETTY WELL DECIDED that Dan didn't intend to tell her anything about his past, when he looked at her again and said, "RCI is flexible when it comes to backgrounds. The concern is more about performance, and I've been getting people—myself included—out of trouble since I was a kid. Do you know New Orleans?" he added.

"I've been there," she told him. "But only once."

"Have you heard of the Irish Channel district?"

"Yes. It's a bit of a rough neighborhood, isn't it?"

"It's only *a bit rough* if you're into serious understatement. Anyway, that's where I grew up. And on my first day of school my older brother gave me a knife to carry. That about sums up the way things were."

"Ah."

"Street smarts and survival skills were more important than anything else. So, as a kid, I learned to do whatever it took to get the results I wanted."

"You didn't exactly follow all the rules, then."

She thought that might make him smile, but he just said, "I didn't exactly follow most of them. You can break a lot of rules, though, without getting caught—or without getting caught very often. At any rate, as soon as I was old enough I joined the police department.''

''From lawbreaker to law enforcer?''

''Uh-huh. I guess that sounds strange to most people, but it isn't. If you're Irish, and from the Channel, you usually end up either a cop or a criminal. It's been that way for so long it's a cliché.''

She nodded. A black Irish family explained the blue eyes and dark hair.

When Dan didn't go on, she said, ''Was your father a cop?''

''No. A couple of my uncles were, though.''

''So you joined the department, and then...''

''Well, that lasted a few years. But I had problems with the rules and regulations, which caused my superiors to have problems with me. And they ended up booting me off the force.''

''Ah,'' she said again, wondering how far someone had to go to get kicked off the NOPD. It was reputed to tolerate more than a few rogue cops.

''Turned out for the best,'' Dan continued, ''because my style is perfect for RCI. The only rule it has is don't let the client get killed.''

She had a sip of champagne, thinking it was no surprise the man wasn't married. People who had problems with rules generally wanted their own way most of the time, which didn't make them good candidates for a partnership.

With an attitude like his, not to mention a job like

his, saying that Dan wouldn't be prime marriage material would be another serious understatement.

Oh, she was sure he was good at his job. And that he took first-rate care of his clients. Otherwise, he wouldn't be with RCI. But when it came to being really deep-down concerned about anyone...well, he probably had the emotional depth of a gnat.

More to check on that assumption than anything else, she said, "Do you get to New Orleans very often these days?"

He shook his head. "My mother died a while back and I was never close to my father."

"And your brother? Or were there more than the two of you?"

"No, just Sean and me. But he isn't living in New Orleans right now."

"Where is he?"

"Your neck of the woods. The San Francisco area."

Dan hesitated, then gave her a what-the-hell sort of look and added, "To be precise, he's doing a stretch in San Quentin for break and enter. He didn't go the cop route. And as it turned out, deciding to try his luck in California was a bad idea."

"Oh."

She took another sip from her glass, surprised that he'd be so forthright about having a convict for a brother. Apparently, Dan O'Neill didn't pull many punches.

Glancing surreptitiously at him, she wondered if

his brother had broken even more of the rules than he or had just gotten caught at it more often.

Not that it mattered. At this point she knew everything she wanted to know—and then some—about her traveling companion.

And she was just as happy that he'd ducked her question about exactly how he'd intended to make the hit man reveal who'd hired him. She doubted she'd have liked the answer.

She stared straight ahead at nothing for a few seconds, then snuck another peak at Dan, unable to deny that she'd been coming around to thinking he was awfully attractive. But now…

Well, he was the sort of man her mother would advise her to run, not walk, away from.

"How about you?" he said.

"How about me, what?"

"What's *your* life story in a hundred words or less?"

"Oh, it's not very interesting."

From here on in, she'd rather keep their relationship as impersonal as possible.

"Everyone's story is interesting."

She doubted that he'd listened to enough of them to know whether that was true.

"So?" he pressed her. "You grew up in San Francisco?"

"No," she said.

Then she told herself not to be rude.

Regardless of anything else, she still owed Dan for giving her an exclusive on Billy. And she shouldn't go out of her way to make their time together unpleasant.

"I grew up in San Luis Obispo," she offered. "Small town in Southern California."

"I've been there. Drove from L.A. to San Francisco a few years ago. San Luis Obispo seemed like a nice place."

"Yes, it is. But with a population of not much more than forty thousand...well, there are a limited number of career opportunities. If I'd stayed, the best I could have hoped for was writing the chamber of commerce's newsletter."

"And you're too ambitious to settle for that."

He shot her a teasing smile, which took her completely by surprise.

It was the first time he'd looked even remotely friendly, and the way her heart reacted by skipping a beat made her nervous.

"Yes, I am," she said. "I've wanted to be a photojournalist for as long as I knew what one was, I guess. When I was little, I was always bugging my brothers to let me take their pictures and interview them."

"I'm sure they liked that."

"Uh-huh, you can just imagine how much. They used to call me Miss Questions, which I hated."

Dan smiled again, and there was even a flicker of warmth in his eyes.

Her heart skipped another beat. She felt more nervous still.

"How many brothers?"

"Three. All older than me."

"So nobody ever picked on you at school."

She almost laughed. Between the two of them, they were racking up understatements at a fast clip.

"That was the upside," she said. "The downside was that, when I was a teenager, none of the boys in my class were brave enough to ask me out. My brothers were on the football and wrestling teams."

"And now?"

She wasn't certain what he meant, and it must have shown, because he added, "I mean, were your brothers all like you? Too ambitious for San Luis Obispo?"

"No, the oldest is still there. He married his high school sweetheart and they have a restaurant. The other two are in L.A. and San Diego. So we're all close enough that it's easy to get together for holidays and whatever."

"May I get you something more to drink?" one of the flight attendants asked.

"Thanks," Dan said. "I wouldn't mind another beer."

"Nothing for me, thanks," Mickey told the woman.

"I'm going to see if I can nap for a bit," she added to Dan. "I didn't get into Victoria until late last night and I was up first thing this morning."

He nodded, reaching for the copy of *Time* he'd bought at the airport.

She closed her eyes, then proceeded to give her heart a stern lecture about inappropriate skipping.

WITH THE FLIGHT TAKING over five hours, and a three-hour time difference, it was long past midnight before Dan felt the plane begin its descent into JFK International.

After raising the shade on his window and having a look out into the night, he turned toward Mickey. There was more than enough light in the darkened cabin to see that she was still asleep.

He let his gaze linger on her generous mouth, then on her eyelashes, dark against her pale skin.

She was a beautiful woman, and he couldn't help wondering, not for the first time, why she wasn't married. Or didn't at least have a boyfriend.

She'd said that she didn't, but there couldn't be too many twenty-nine-year old women—he'd learned her age, along with a few other facts, while checking her ID—who looked like her and were walking around unattached.

Of course, that was likely just an at-this-particular-moment-in-time circumstance. Unless she put men second to her job and ambition.

Maybe she did, but the possibility was pure speculation. And why was he speculating about her personal life, anyway?

That wasn't exactly a tough question to answer.

She was so damn gutsy that, when she wasn't busy being manipulative Miss Questions, he actually kind of liked her. And when it came to the way she looked and smelled…

Hell, just watching her sleep, with her hair tousled

and her entire body relaxed, was enough to make him imagine her in bed beside him.

That, however, wasn't a good thing to be imagining. Especially not when there was no way he'd ever find himself sleeping with her.

Unless his read of her was totally wrong, Mickey Westover wasn't into casual sex. And since he wasn't into anything more than that… Oh, he didn't see anything wrong with commitment. It just wasn't for him.

His life simply didn't lend itself to serious relationships with women, so the only ones he had were brief and to the point.

He turned back toward the window, telling himself that—regardless of anything else—he and Mickey weren't going to be together long enough for anything to develop.

She'd only be with him until he got this situation with Billy sorted out, and he intended to do that very quickly.

With any luck, Ken had located Billy by now. And even if he hadn't, they'd nab him when he arrived at the TV studio. He was still hoping it wouldn't come to that, though, because once Billy made up his mind about something he could be damn stubborn.

And if he was practically on the set of the show before they caught up with him, he'd be bound and determined to go ahead with his appearance.

So there they'd be, standing in front of NBS…

Man, he really didn't like the possibility of ending

up totally exposed on the street—trying to make Billy agree to get the hell out of there, while at the same time watching every which way for the killer. And if the hit man was there…well, if that happened, and he and Billy were a couple of talking targets, the situation could get really nasty.

That thought made him look at Mickey again.

If they did have to catch up with Billy at the studio, she couldn't come along. Not when there'd be the risk of a shoot-out.

He knew she'd give him an argument. And remind him, one more time, that she'd been a big help back at Billy's place. Which was precisely why he didn't intend to raise the subject until after he'd talked to Ken again.

Hell, he'd probably be wise not to say anything until he absolutely had to. Until he was practically on his way to NBS, assuming that was how this played out. Then Mickey wouldn't have time to argue.

But maybe he was worrying for nothing. If Ken had already found Billy there'd be no need to say anything to her. Ever.

He had a strong feeling their star was still on the loose, though. And if that was the case…well, he just wasn't going to let Mickey walk into a potentially dangerous situation. Regardless of how much fuss she put up.

He and Ken would handle things on their own. They'd get Billy safely back under wraps, then it would be a matter of figuring out who the hit man was and who'd hired him. Two pieces of information he'd already have if Mickey hadn't blown his decoy plan.

He looked away from her once more and stared down at the lights of New York, assuring himself that things were still going to work out just fine.

This wasn't the first job he'd done that had gotten more complicated than it should have. And in due course, he'd turn up one of those two facts he needed.

Whichever piece of the puzzle he came up with first would give him the other one. Then it would be case closed.

Mickey would have her scoop and he'd never see her again. She'd go back to San Francisco. And to San Luis Obispo—*for holidays and whatever,* as she'd put it.

His thoughts drifted to how different her upbringing must have been from his. At least as different, he imagined, as the lives they led now. Not that he really knew much about her life, but…

He found himself eyeing her yet again.

With her hair mussed and any makeup she'd been wearing long gone, she looked the picture of innocence curled up beside him. Not like an ambitious career woman, but like a little girl whose brothers had nicknamed her Miss Questions.

He wondered if they still called her that. If they teased her when the family got together.

He'd bet they did.

Leaning back in his seat, he tried not to think

about the last time he'd seen his family. It had been at his mother's funeral.

His brother had been there. Escorted by a prison guard. And their father had been his usual charming self. After the ceremony, the old man had gotten into a row with a couple of the relatives and Dan had come within an inch of decking him.

But instead of doing that, he'd just said a quiet goodbye to Sean and left. He hadn't been back to New Orleans since.

"We're landing," Mickey murmured.

"Uh-huh," he said, looking at her once more and thinking that—even half asleep—she looked sexy as hell.

"I didn't dream I'd sleep so long."

"You didn't miss anything," he told her.

Then he watched her slowly comb her fingers through her long hair, aware that for some reason he was feeling empty inside.

WHILE DAN SPOKE on his cell phone with Ken Heath, Mickey stood next to him watching for their cases.

Nothing had appeared on the carousel yet, but he'd said theirs would be among the first out, one of the perks of traveling first class.

Not that they had much luggage.

Aside from her camera and laptop, her only bag was the carry-on she routinely used for out-of-town assignments. Even ones that were supposed to be just day trips. She'd been stranded often enough that she always packed basic essentials and extra clothes in the small bag.

Usually she kept it with her, which saved time at the arrivals end. But she'd checked it on this flight, figuring that since they'd have to wait for Dan's case there was no point in hauling hers on and off the plane.

Dan's case. Which contained his Glock and the killer's Magnum, as well as the gun she'd found in the drawer at Billy's.

Glancing at Dan, she thought back to the argument they'd had about bringing it along.

The Magnum was far too big for her to handle easily, so she'd simply assumed he'd stick Billy's semiautomatic in his suitcase for her—assumed it once he'd eventually agreed to let her go with him, that was.

But he'd said no way. That he didn't want her carrying a gun. Then he'd given her his this-isn't-open-for-discussion line again, telling her that New York had strict gun laws and she'd be breaking them if she was armed.

The same didn't apply to him, however.

He'd finally explained why he was allowed to take guns on commercial flights, as well as why he could carry them, without possessing a state license, in most parts of the country.

Risk Control International, he'd said, had an arrangement with the federal aviation people and most of the state governments.

But regardless of the fact that RCI's arrangement

didn't cover her, she certainly didn't want to be unarmed if they encountered their killer a second time.

To her, that had seemed like an excellent point. Dan, though, had said that if she shot anyone—even if it was a professional hit man—she'd end up behind bars.

However, when she'd asked how he'd feel if she got herself killed because she was defenseless, he'd caved.

At the time, she'd been surprised.

Now, after he'd told her enough about himself that she knew he had a rules-were-made-for-breaking approach to life, she was surprised he'd bothered arguing at all.

Turning her thoughts back to the moment, she tuned into Dan's phone conversation again.

Hearing only one side of it wasn't enabling her to put everything together, but she was pretty sure that Ken Heath still hadn't located Billy.

If she was right, it would mean defaulting to Plan B and intercepting him when he arrived at the TV studio.

But if the killer had learned Billy was going to be Sherry Sherman's guest…

Well, if he had, and if Dan could not only prevent him from killing Billy but also keep him from making good his escape this time, then—as Dan had put it—the situation would be resolved. And she'd be filing her exclusive.

Just as she felt herself getting excited about that

prospect all over again, Dan said into the phone, "All right. Exactly where is NBS?"

Okay. So they were going with Plan B.

"And you've checked the layout?" he asked Ken. "Is there a back way in?"

There was a brief pause, then he said, "Fine. I'll cover the front street. I'll watch for Billy and for anyone hanging around. You keep an eye on the back in case our friend shows up there."

He listened for a few seconds before saying, "I know it's not. But if this guy's good he'll be thinking outside the box, so we've got to cover all the bases. I just wish I could give you a better description of him, but…"

After listening again, he glanced at Mickey and said, "Do you know anything about TV talk shows?"

She nodded. "I've interviewed a few hosts."

"How long before airtime do the guests arrive?"

"At least an hour. Usually, it's more like ninety minutes. They need time to get made up, then the host chats with them in the green room for a bit."

"She says ninety minutes," he told Ken. "But to be safe we'd better get there by seven.

"I'll phone you once I have Billy," he added. "Or if I run into a problem."

By *problem,* of course, he meant that they might not be the only ones waiting out front to intercept Billy. And if the killer was there, he'd be planning to do his intercepting with bullets.

While that disconcerting thought was flitting

through her head, her carry-on appeared, with Dan's suitcase close behind it.

When she glanced at him, he nodded that he'd spotted them, too. He quickly finished up his conversation with Ken and grabbed them off the conveyor belt.

"So?" she said, adjusting the strap of her camera bag as they started off.

"Well, Ken called it a night an hour ago. He decided it was late enough that Billy wouldn't still be hitting the clubs. Not when he's figuring he has to look good for TV in a few hours."

"And Ken has no idea where he'd be staying?"

"He's got some ideas, but they wouldn't get us anywhere. If he booked into a hotel he'll have used an alias. And if he's staying with someone he knows...well, there's no point phoning a bunch of people in the middle of the night."

"Then there's nothing we can do but wait for morning," Mickey concluded.

"It won't be much of a wait," Dan said, glancing at his watch. "But yeah, that's what we have to do. And we might as well get ourselves a couple of rooms. Even a little rest would make me more alert."

She nodded. She'd slept for long enough on the plane that she wasn't feeling too bad. Dan, however, looked half-dead, which was easily understandable.

He'd mentioned that he'd been glued to those monitors in Billy's retreat for almost forty-eight hours before she'd arrived. And she had a feeling that if he'd managed to get any sleep during their flight it hadn't been much.

They reached the sliding glass doors, headed out of the terminal and grabbed a taxi.

"Downtown Manhattan," Dan told the cabbie. "And is there a hotel near the NBS studio that you'd recommend?"

The man glanced at them in the rearview mirror. "You care if it's real fancy?"

"No. As long as it's half-decent."

"I can call the desk at one I'm thinking of," he said, picking up a cell phone from the seat beside him. "See if there's anything available."

"Thanks, that would be great."

As they sped through the darkness, Mickey couldn't help thinking that even though New York was known as the city that never sleeps it was awfully quiet in the middle of the night.

There was so little traffic that the trip from the airport didn't take nearly as long as she'd expected.

The driver dropped them off at an old but seemingly well maintained hotel not far from Times Square.

Inside, the desk clerk—who was watching a movie on a small television set behind the counter—didn't look happy when they interrupted his viewing.

"Our cabbie phoned about us," Dan told him, producing a credit card. "We need two rooms."

"Oh. He didn't say that. And I only have one left. We booked in a convention overflow earlier."

He glanced at his computer, then added, "The room I've got has two beds."

Dan looked at Mickey.

"Does it have a data port?" she asked the clerk.

"Uh-huh."

"Then fine," she said.

As long as she'd easily be able to e-mail an article and pictures to the *Post* if she needed to, she'd rather not waste time looking for another hotel.

"These convention people took us by surprise, and that's my last registration card," the man said, handing it to Dan. "So would you mind just filling it out as Mr. and Mrs.?"

Mickey eyed him, wondering why Dan shouldn't either just leave her off entirely or squeeze both their names onto it.

She was going to ask, but the man had already turned his attention back to the movie. Besides, why should she care what the rules were for registering in New York hotels?

While Dan wrote and she waited, she began thinking that the Mr. and Mrs. bit was positively laughable.

She'd met Dan O'Neill less than twenty-four hours ago, and aside from what he'd told her on the plane she knew absolutely nothing about him.

She didn't even have any idea where he lived. Or maybe he just went from job to job, staying in whatever city the current one took him to.

It was hard for her to imagine what that sort of life would be like. No roots, no sense of belonging someplace. And he'd said he wasn't close to his family.

Actually, everything she *did* know about him suggested they were nothing at all alike.

But what did that matter when their relationship was strictly business?

While the desk clerk slapped down a card-key and said, "Eight-zero-three," an imaginary voice was saying, *Strictly business?*

Then it went on to remind her that, mere hours ago, she'd been thinking Dan was awfully cute.

She told it to be quiet.

After all, she'd only been attracted to him briefly.

And only before she'd discovered that he wasn't even remotely her type. That he lived life by his own rules, which she wouldn't be at all shocked to learn he made up as he went along.

Lord, Daniel O'Neill wouldn't be *any* woman's type.

Not unless the woman in question was either insane or a masochist.

CHAPTER SIX

FOR A FEW DISORIENTED SECONDS, Mickey had no idea what she was doing in a strange bed. Or why she was wearing her exercise shorts and T-shirt.

Then, as the digital number on the clock radio changed from 5:49 a.m. to 5:50 a.m., she realized she was in New York. In a hotel room.

As more recollections drifted back, she remembered that, after a post-check-in shower, she'd decided against wearing her somewhat skimpy nightshirt because she was sharing the room with Daniel O'Neill.

Yes. In the early-morning haze she could see that he was asleep in the other bed.

And across the room, she could make out the desk she'd set her laptop on, by the data port she'd been concerned about having.

While she finished waking up, her eyes filled in the remaining details. The other furniture consisted of a round coffee table and a couple of the kind of tub chairs that were endemic to hotel rooms everywhere—lightweight ones that were easy to move, which always made her wonder if decorators figured that a lot of hotel guests were into rearranging their surroundings.

As the time changed to 5:51 a.m., she recalled Dan requesting a six-o'clock wake-up call. And that, before he'd collapsed into bed, he'd set the alarm for good measure.

But she'd known that she wouldn't need either. Whenever she had an important reason for waking up, her internal alarm went off ten minutes early. And getting her story on Billy Brent was a *very* important reason.

Once the cobwebs had completely finished clearing from her brain, she swung her legs over the side of the bed. Then she sat looking at Dan.

A slice of morning light was slanting into the room through a space between the drapes and falling across his face.

He was badly overdue for a shave, but he didn't seem like nearly such a tough guy when he was asleep. And with the sunlight softening his features, he looked…

She tried to be objective. If she didn't know what she knew about him, would she find him sexy or not?

Bad question, she realized as a curl of warmth started low in her belly.

Telling herself she was just hungry, she grabbed her carry-on and quietly headed for the bathroom. Since she'd showered just a couple of hours ago, she only needed a few minutes now and was back in the main room, wearing her jeans and an oversize shirt by the time the alarm went off.

Dan twitched and mumbled something, then buried his head under the pillow.

She turned off the alarm and waited a few seconds. When he didn't move again, she said, "Dan, it's six o'clock."

The phone began ringing, so she answered it and thanked the desk clerk for calling, then said, "You have to get up."

"Two minutes," he said, his voice thick.

She sat down on the edge of her bed and gave him the best part of his two minutes before saying, "Billy Brent. Hit man. NBS studio by seven o'clock."

He made a Neanderthal-like noise, then shoved back the blankets and crawled out of bed.

He'd slept in his underwear; his early-morning erection was impossible to ignore.

Swallowing hard, she looked away. But her eyes double-crossed her as he started for the bathroom and she couldn't stop her gaze from following him.

His bare back was so well muscled it almost made her fingers itch. And that tight butt, with his briefs clinging to it, started her thinking thoughts she definitely didn't want to be thinking.

Not about him.

Before he could close the bathroom door, she said, "I noticed a twenty-four-hour deli across the street. Why don't I go get us some coffee and muffins."

"Good idea," he told her.

A few seconds later, he'd shut the door and water began running in the shower.

The sound made her mind conjure up an image of Daniel O'Neill naked.

She seriously wished it hadn't—and not because it repulsed her.

THE DELI PROVED to be surprisingly busy, which meant that Mickey took a little longer getting back to the room than she'd anticipated. By the time she returned, Dan had shaved and dressed and was looking like a real person rather than a zombie.

He didn't look quite like himself, though. He was wearing a baseball cap, which hid his short hair, and a bomber jacket with the collar turned up.

"What do you think of my disguise?" he asked. "Figure I'll be able to get close to Billy before he realizes it's me?"

"And you want to do that because...?"

He shrugged. "I figure he'll give me an argument about canceling on Sherry Sherman. And if he notices me coming, he might just take off into the studio and sic NBS security on me."

"He'd do that?"

"In a heartbeat. So? The disguise? Does it work?"

She gave him an appraising once-over.

Even this early in the morning he was going to be hot in that jacket, but the collar did conceal part of his face. And the sunglasses he was holding would help, too.

"I guess it'll depend on how closely Billy's paying attention," she said.

"I'm probably okay there. He's not a morning person."

Dan seemed about to say something more, but when he didn't she dug her wallet and cell phone out of her purse.

It wasn't until she glanced at the cellular's little screen, and saw it was indicating imminent death, that she realized she should have plugged it into its charger after they'd checked in.

"Rats," she muttered, thinking she must have been more tired than she'd realized.

"What?" Dan said.

"My phone's run down. I'll have to leave it charging while we're gone."

She quickly plugged it in, then stashed her wallet into her camera bag and locked her purse inside her carry-on.

With her camera and laptop, she'd have enough to keep track of without a purse. And given the choice between toting it or her laptop, the computer was an easy winner.

She could do without the accumulation of junk in her purse, but when she might find herself face-to-face with a fast-breaking story...

The anticipation of that made her really want to get a move on, so she picked up the deli bag and said "If we're going to be there by seven, should we just take this with us?"

Dan hesitated a moment before saying, "Mickey, you have to stay here."

She stared at him, momentarily expecting him to tell her he was just joking.

When he didn't, the longer the silence stretched the angrier she grew.

"We have a deal," she said at last.

"Right, we do. And the deal is that you get an exclusive. I never said—"

"Don't think for one second that I'm staying here," she interrupted. "I remember exactly what you said. And what I said. I said I'd get the story *firsthand,* which would save both of us time. And you never said that wasn't the way it would be. So don't start thinking that—"

"Look," he snapped, "if the hit man's there this will be dangerous."

"And what am I? A cream puff? Dan, do you how many journalists were killed last year?"

"I have no idea."

"Fewer than fifty. Worldwide. In an entire year."

"You have a statistic like that at your fingertips? Don't you think that's just a little morbid? Or maybe even warped?"

"Don't try to change the subject. Fifty is practically the same as zero."

He muttered, "I assume math was never your best subject."

She gave him a black look before saying, "Mathematically speaking, I'm probably in more danger just by visiting New York City than by covering this story. And reporting news is what journalists do. They cover wars and insurrections and riots and—"

"Arts and Entertainment journalists don't."

"That's exactly my point! If I'm not right there on the scene, the brass at the *Post* won't be half as impressed. And all we're talking about is one man with a gun. A man who wants to kill Billy Brent, not me. Besides, we're not even sure he'll show up," she added. "This story might turn out to be nothing more than you stopping Billy from appearing on Sherry Sherman because his life's in danger. Not that I'm saying a superstar's life being at risk isn't front-page news, but—"

"No," Dan interrupted firmly. "The odds are too high that our guy *will* show up. So I am *not* having you with me."

"Fine."

"What do you mean, *fine?*"

When he eyed her suspiciously, she shrugged, doing her best to look cool even though she was seething inside.

"I mean, if you don't want me with you then I'll go by myself. I can take my own cab, Dan."

"Oh, no. That is not going to happen."

"You think not? And how are you going to prevent it? By tying me up?"

"Now there's an idea."

"Listen to me, Daniel O'Neill. You try anything like that and I'll scream so loudly nobody will have to call the cops. They'll hear me from the nearest precinct."

She dug his coffee and one of the muffins from the bag and slammed them down on the bedside table so hard the coffee would have been all over the floor if not for the lid.

Then she grabbed her camera bag and laptop, turned on her heel and marched out of the hotel room.

For a good ten seconds after Mickey was gone, Dan simply stood swearing to himself. And *at* himself.

What on earth had made him figure he'd tell her to stay here and she would? It must have been lack of sleep. When he'd been thinking about this last night he'd been bone tired. Hell, never mind bone tired. He must have been virtually brain-dead. He knew the woman didn't listen.

So now what did he do?

She was going to be at NBS whether he liked it or not. And as much as he *didn't* like it, she'd be safer if she was near enough that he could keep a close eye on her.

Briefly he wondered why he even cared whether she got herself shot. After all, she was such a pain in the butt she practically deserved to.

Then he realized this was exactly what he'd known would happen. He'd let a civilian come along on a job—which had been utter stupidity on his part—and now he felt responsible for her safety.

He also felt like kicking himself.

Settling for simply swearing under his breath, he started after her.

A SHORT AND SILENT cab ride later, Mickey and Dan were in position on Fifth Avenue, outside the NBS building. She had her laptop slung over one shoulder, her camera bag over the other and her Nikon out. Whatever happened, she was ready for it.

Of course, trying to get her pictures while she was loaded down like a pack mule was hardly ideal. But this was Manhattan. If she put anything on the sidewalk and took her eyes off it for three seconds, it would vanish.

As she shifted her weight from one foot to the other, her nervous energy not letting her stand still, she was very aware of Billy's semiautomatic nudging her stomach. She'd tucked it out of sight beneath her shirt and was surprised that Dan hadn't asked what she'd done with it.

Undoubtedly, though, that was only because he hadn't asked her *anything*. In fact, he'd spoken precisely three words to her since he'd caught up with her outside the hotel.

"Okay, you win," he'd muttered.

That had been it.

She glanced at him and saw that the blood red aura of anger was still spiking in flashes around him—although the smoke had finally stopped coming out of his ears.

But what gave him any more right than she had to be angry?

Nothing.

Because they'd made a deal. And she hated people who welched on deals.

Especially ones like this. Ones that could affect her entire professional future.

She ordered herself to stop thinking about Dan being a welcher and focus her attention completely on the moment.

If she was she going to write a slam-dunk of a story, she couldn't miss any important details, which meant that she'd better organize her thoughts and start making some mental notes.

Dan had already been on the phone with Ken Heath, so they knew he was in place, covering the building's back entrance. Mickey thought about that for a minute, but the idea of their hit man targeting Billy *inside* still didn't make much sense to her. Surely it would be a lot easier for a killer to manage a safe getaway if he was on the street to begin with.

But when she'd voiced her thoughts to Dan, he'd told her never to assume she could figure out how a contract killer would think. That it was a sure way of screwing up. And that, given the big picture, Ken was in the best place.

As for Dan and her, they were well enough concealed behind one of the building's stone pillars that if the killer *was* on the street, he'd be unlikely to spot them.

As for Billy, since he'd never laid eyes on her she was immaterial to that equation.

She took a slow, deep breath, telling herself there was nothing to do now but wait. Less than a minute later, she realized how hard the wait was going to be.

The city was already alive with New Yorkers making their way to work, and each time a taxi pulled up at the curb she glanced anxiously along the sidewalk, looking for anyone else who might be interested in the identity of its passenger. But if the hit man was here, he wasn't obvious.

When yet another taxi stopped, she had a feeling that this one was Billy's—until a woman climbed out.

"I doubt he'll arrive by cab," Dan said.

"Oh?" She glanced at him, surprised that his tone had been verging on civil.

He let a beat or two pass, then said, "Look, you know I'm not happy that you're here, but since you are we've got to call a truce. Because if our guy *does* turn up…well, if I tell you to do something, you're going to have to do it. Fast. Without trying to second-guess me. Okay?"

She briefly considered that. As much as she didn't like blindly following orders, Dan was an expert when it came to this sort of thing. She was anything but.

"Okay," she agreed.

"Where's your gun?"

"Right here under my shirt," she said, patting her waist.

"Well no matter what happens, leave it there unless *your* life's in danger."

"But—"

"No *buts,* Mickey. Billy's safety is my responsibility, not yours."

She hesitated, then nodded, knowing he was right, and very aware that her anxiety level had just notched up even higher than it had already been.

Despite what she'd told him earlier, at the moment "fewer than fifty" dead journalists no longer seemed practically the same as zero at all.

"Now, as I was saying," he continued, "Billy probably won't arrive by cab. He's far more likely to have hired a limo."

"And draw attention to himself? Even though he knows someone's out to kill him?"

"Uh-huh. He'd be more worried about fans seeing him in a taxi. Like a mere mortal."

"He needs to get his priorities straight," she said, looking along the sidewalk once again.

But what did she really expect to see?

Back at Billy's retreat, the killer had gotten a good look at both Dan *and* her. So if he did spot them here, he'd recognize them right off—or recognize her, at least, depending on how effective Dan's disguise was.

But they didn't have the same advantage.

Every second man on the street was average height and average weight. So the hit man could be shoulder to shoulder with her and she wouldn't realize it was him.

Not unless he was wearing his rubber mask again. And that wasn't going to happen.

Even in New York, at least a few people would take notice of a mask. And while Billy might be crazy enough to draw attention to himself, a contract killer would go out of his way not to.

"Do you think he's here?" she asked Dan.

He shrugged. "I figure the odds are better than fifty-fifty. If he's good at what he does, he'll have learned that Billy's supposed to be on that show."

Better than fifty-fifty.

She had a horrible feeling that was Dan's way of saying he figured the odds were awfully high.

She scanned the street again, then told herself that it was an exercise in futility.

If their guy *was* here, wouldn't he be out of sight? Standing in a nearby doorway? Or maybe even behind another of the pillars? Watching and waiting, just as they were?

Absently she rested her hand against the bulge of Billy's gun, reflecting that she'd never shot at anything except targets. Not until yesterday, and even then she'd only fired into the air.

She was in the process of warning herself that wasn't a good thing to be thinking about when Dan said, "This might be Billy now."

Her gaze darted to the street.

Spotting a black stretch limo crawling along the block toward them started her heart beating triple time.

"It could be Sherry Sherman," Dan said. "Or one of the other guests."

"Right," she agreed. It was Billy Brent, though. She simply knew it was.

"But I'm going to get a little closer to the curb,"

Dan added. "Just in case. You stay behind that pillar where you'll be safe. You can take your pictures from there, right?"

"Sure."

She *could,* but she wouldn't.

However, she certainly wasn't about to tell *him* that she had no intention of limiting herself by staying put, that she had to get absolutely great shots, because at least a couple of them were bound to end up on the *Post*'s front page.

"If there's any excitement, keep under cover," Dan said, drawing her attention back to him. "And if I get the sense that my best move is to just take off with Billy, we'll meet up back at the hotel. Got it?"

She nodded. If there was any excitement, though, she intended to be capturing it with her camera.

Even if there wasn't any, she needed good pictures of Billy's arrival. Of Dan hustling him back into that stretch because a killer might be lying in wait for him.

As she stood watching the street, captions began popping into her head.

Billy Brent Ignores Death Threat

Superstar Billy Brent, Living In Mortal Danger

Billy Brent Stalked By A Killer

When the limo pulled up to the curb, she put a lid on the captions and focused her camera.

Luck was on her side. She only needed to move inches from the protection of the pillar to get the angle she wanted.

A uniformed man climbed out and started around the front of his stretch.

Mickey quickly glanced either way but saw nothing out of the ordinary. When she looked back toward the limo, Dan was casually closing in on it.

The darkly tinted windows would prevent him from seeing whoever was inside until the passenger's door was open, so he wasn't bothering to try. Instead, he kept his gaze on the pavement as he moved forward, seemingly so lost in thought that he wasn't even aware of the vehicle's existence.

When the driver reached for the door handle, Dan turned as if he'd heard someone call his name from behind. Actually, Mickey knew, he was doing a final check along the street.

The driver opened the door.

His passenger began to climb out.

The instant Mickey saw that it *was* Billy she started getting her shots.

Then Dan was in her viewfinder, blocking Billy from her sight and shoving him back into the vehicle.

Quickly he climbed in after him.

Dan had obviously said something to the driver, because the man raced around to the far side again. A moment later, the limo pulled away from the curb.

As it joined the flow of traffic, Mickey took a final couple of shots. Then she lowered her camera and slowly scanned the sidewalk in front of NBS.

At least a few people had probably noticed what had just happened, but nobody was looking curiously after the stretch as it made its way down the street.

Of course, New Yorkers were a breed apart, as the saying went. It would take a lot more than a limo coming and going—even with a little unusual activity—to attract much attention on Fifth Avenue.

She was just about to put her camera away when she realized a man, standing about thirty feet along the sidewalk, was staring at her, his expression filled with a cold certainty of recognition.

Seeing him sent a chill through her.

He was wearing a lightweight beige jacket, and when he reached inside it the movement was so casual it was almost in slow motion. But she knew he was going for a gun.

The chill became a flash freeze inside her veins, because even though every second man on the street was average height and average weight, she didn't have the slightest doubt about this particular one's identity.

CHAPTER SEVEN

''JUST BE SURE Sherry knows that I feel absolutely terrible about leaving her in the lurch,'' Billy said into the phone. ''But I'm so sick I could hardly get out of bed to call her.''

Dan, sitting in one of the hotel room's tub chairs and listening, couldn't help thinking that the man was a damn good actor.

People, himself included, tended to think of Billy Brent as pure Hollywood. To forget that he'd started out in legitimate theater and spent a lot of years paying his dues in both On- and Off-Broadway theaters before the film industry had ''discovered'' him.

In any event, at the moment he was giving a Tony-winning performance. He not only sounded as if he honestly *was* tremendously sorry, but as if he was at death's door to boot.

After a pause, he said, ''Yeah, thanks, I'm sure I'll be okay in a few days.''

Once he'd hung up, he scowled across the room.

''Don't look at me like that,'' Dan told him. ''Would you rather I'd let you out onto the street? So he could shoot you?''

''You're certain he was there?''

"Isn't that what I said?"

Of course, in truth, he wasn't at all sure the hit man had been waiting outside the studio. He'd simply seen the argumentative expression on Billy's face and gone with his instinct to shove him back into the limo.

That done, he'd claimed that he'd spotted the killer at the very last second, when it had been too late to even try to do anything but get Billy out of there. And, all in all, the end result had been pretty good.

Billy was safe for the moment, and was also basically convinced that he'd come within an inch of being killed, which should make him far less inclined to even think about taking off again.

In the short term, at least. Until he got back to thinking he was Billy the Invincible.

When the man wordlessly turned and headed into the bathroom, Dan took his cellular phone from his belt and punched in Ken Heath's number, hoping against hope that Ken had Mickey with him by now.

As soon as the limo had pulled away from NBS, he'd called Ken and told him to head around to the front of the building and connect with her, which shouldn't have been at all tough.

Even though the two of them had never met, there'd been only one knock-'em-dead-looking woman out there wearing jeans and a white shirt. Not to mention loaded down with a camera bag and laptop.

But Ken had called back a few minutes later to say there was no sign of her.

And since she hadn't shown up here, where on earth was she?

The very last thing he'd told her was that if he decided it would be best to just take off with Billy, she should meet up with them back at the hotel.

So why wasn't she here? Or why hadn't she at least phoned?

He glanced at her cellular, still plugged into its charger. But pay phones weren't an extinct species.

"Find her?" he quietly asked when Ken answered his phone.

"Haven't even found a trace," Ken told him. "Want me to keep looking?"

"No, she could be anywhere by now, so you might as well come and take Billy off my hands."

"On my way," he said, his words accompanied by the sound of Billy flushing.

Dan clicked off and had his phone clipped back on his belt before Billy strolled out of the bathroom.

He looked around the room and said, "She's still not here?"

His annoyed expression made Dan wish he'd never mentioned Mickey, but he'd had no choice since she was supposed to have arrived long before this.

Resisting the urge to ask if Billy figured Mickey had gotten here and was hiding in the closet, Dan merely shook his head.

"Then where is she?" Billy demanded.

"I don't know," he said, back to seriously wishing he did. He wasn't at all happy that he'd only been able to come up with two possible answers. And he didn't like either of them.

But either something had happened to Mickey after he and Billy had left the scene, or she wasn't coming back to the hotel until she'd e-mailed a damned article to the *Post.*

When his mind began to focus on the first possibility, he tried not to let it. Because if the killer had been at NBS, and he'd spotted her, she could easily be dead.

The chance of that made him icy cold inside, which was hardly surprising. From the outset, he'd realized that he'd feel responsible for her if he let her come along. And that he'd blame himself if anything happened to her. But...

Oh, hell. As much as he'd rather not admit it, he knew he wasn't worrying about her only out of a sense of responsibility.

Maybe he didn't really *want* to like Mickey Westover. And he knew the fact that he kind of did might not be good. But regardless of what he wanted or knew, there was just something about her that he couldn't *help* liking.

Maybe, aside from her gutsiness, the draw was that she reminded him a little of himself. Once he set a goal, he reached it, regardless of what obstacles were in the way. And Mickey was being just as pigheaded about getting her story.

Well, pigheaded was hardly a trait most people would find admirable. So that probably wasn't the best word to use, especially not if he was talking to her.

Determined.

Uh-huh, that was better. He couldn't help admiring her determination. Being forced to deal with it, however, was an entirely different story.

That, he didn't like one bit.

Even so, if anything awful had happened to her...

He reminded himself that she'd had Billy's gun.

But what good would it have been to her if she'd come up against a contract killer?

Absolutely none.

No amount of target practice with her brothers would have prepared her to face off against a professional hit man.

Of course, as she, herself, had said, the guy was after Billy, not her.

Only what if she'd done something crazy?

Man, oh, man, he didn't even want to imagine what that woman might have decided to do. Or what it could have led to. Trying to take his mind off his imaginings, he shifted his gaze to the television, whispering away in the corner.

He'd flicked it on when they came in and tuned it to a local channel, on the theory that if anyone had been shot on Fifth Avenue they'd have interrupted their regular programming for a report.

But what if the killer had simply grabbed Mickey? Forced her to go with him?

Dan tried desperately to force those thoughts from his head. He'd always found there was a great deal of merit to that approach, despite what a psychiatrist would undoubtedly say to the contrary.

"You know how I am," Billy said.

Dan looked over at him.

"Once I've made a decision I like to move on it. Right away."

Billy paused, obviously waiting for a complimentary remark about his decisive nature.

Dan had pegged the trait more as indicating an impulsive personality, but he humored the guy and said, "Uh-huh."

"So now that you've made me realize I have to stay out of sight until you've tracked this killer down," Billy continued, "I want to head back to New England. You *are* sure I'll be safe there, right?"

"Perfectly. And you'll be on your way in no time. Ken should get here in just a few minutes, then the two of you can take off."

"Good," Billy said.

Picking up the TV remote, he bumped up the volume to ear shattering.

As he began channel surfing, Mickey was suddenly front and center in Dan's mind again. And he was right back to worrying that something horrible had happened to her.

He didn't want to even consider why that might be, because the most obvious reason was that he was falling for her, and he definitely wasn't.

Oh, he'd concede that, for whatever reasons, he did like her some—even though she could be as annoying as hell. *Liking,* however, was a long, long way from *falling.*

And he couldn't possibly be falling for her because he never let *any* woman get to him that way, let alone a stubborn and manipulative one.

He silently repeated that a couple of times, uneasily thinking there might be a flaw in the logic.

Then he realized what it was.

Mickey Westover wasn't just *any* woman.

In fact, she was unique. He'd never met anyone else quite like her.

And if he wasn't falling for her, then why was he so darned concerned about her that he felt as if a large rodent was busily gnawing at his insides? And why, more than anything else, did he wish she was back here with him so he'd know she was safe?

He took a deep breath, then exhaled slowly, aware of just how much he didn't want to be feeling the way he did.

Emotions only complicated things. They got in the way of sane, rational thought.

And aside from that—assuming Mickey wasn't lying dead someplace—having an emotional pull toward her would only make the rest of the time he had to spend with her awkward as hell. Because there was no way in the world he intended to act on feelings he didn't want to have.

End of story.

Except that he simply couldn't stop worrying about her.

He told himself that she seemed pretty good at

taking care of herself. Very good, actually, which meant he was probably worrying for nothing. But if that was the case, it left him with his single alternative explanation for why she wasn't here.

Glancing at the data port on the desk, he vaguely recalled her asking the desk clerk if the room had one. Obviously, she'd figured that she'd need it.

Yet, realistically, there was no reason she'd have had to come back here to file a story. This was Manhattan, where there were Internet cafés on every second block. So she might not only have already written her article, it might already be at the *Post.*

However, surely that wasn't likely.

After all, he reminded himself, Lydia had said Mickey Westover was a woman who kept her word. So, since Lydia was never wrong…

Only nobody was *never* wrong.

And Mickey was so damned determined to get her byline on the front page…

They'd made a deal, though, which she'd reminded him about often enough that its terms were etched on his brain.

In exchange for her exclusive, she'd agreed that she wouldn't breathe a word to her paper about anything to do with Billy until he was safe and the hit man had been taken care of.

But what if her ambition had gotten the better of her?

Dammit, that would be all he needed.

His job was to establish who'd put the contract out on Billy and to prevent him from ending up dead.

And if the whole world found out a contract killer was targeting their superstar, the killer would drop so far out of sight that finding him would be impossible even if Dan *did* learn who was behind the contract.

Of course, the killer would only go into hiding temporarily.

He'd been paid to whack Billy, so he wouldn't give up until he'd either done that or died trying. Otherwise, his reputation would be in the toilet.

And whoever he was, he'd be a damned sight more patient than Billy, who—regardless of what he was saying at the moment—wouldn't be back in New England with Ken for more than a couple of days before he got cabin fever.

The longer Billy was forced to hide out, the more he'd rationalize away the danger. And if he took off on Ken again, they might not be as lucky next time.

Wearily shaking his head, Dan strode across to the window and stared down at the street, as if by looking out he could magically make Mickey appear.

But it wasn't her he saw getting out of a cab. It was a man.

And although he couldn't be positive from eight floors up, he was pretty sure it was Ken Heath.

Ken looked cautiously in either direction, then hurried across the sidewalk to the hotel's entrance.

DAN WAS TRYING to decide just how long he should stay in the hotel room hoping that Mickey would show.

If she didn't, he'd eventually have to go looking for her even though it would be like searching for the proverbial needle.

He was in the midst of recalling that he'd just known she'd be trouble if he let her come along, when someone knocked.

That sound was immediately followed by the woman, herself, saying, "Dan? It's me."

The awareness that he'd never been so relieved in his entire life was extremely unsettling.

He told himself, definitely not for the first time, that regardless of what feelings he might think he'd been developing toward Mickey, the only smart course of action was to pay no attention to them. Then he opened the door to her, and those feelings he so badly wanted to ignore threatened to overwhelm him.

He simply stood staring at her for a moment. Her hair was tousled, her face was covered by a sheen of perspiration and she looked decidedly frazzled.

She also looked utterly gorgeous.

Somehow, that last thought succeeded in scuttling through his mind before he could manage to stop it.

"Where the hell have you been?" he greeted her.

"It's nice to see you again, too," she said, stepping inside and closing the door.

"Okay. Sorry. It's just that I was getting a little concerned."

"Really?"

When she smiled, he mentally kicked himself. He hadn't meant to admit that.

"Where's Billy?" she asked, glancing around.

"On his way back to where we were keeping him. Ken just picked him up."

She looked disappointed that she wasn't about to meet their superstar, but that was the least of Dan's worries.

"What took you so long?" he said.

"I used a circuitous route."

"A circuitous route? You've had time to see half the city. Or did your route involve a stop at an Internet café?"

She eyed him coldly for a moment, then said, "What are you suggesting?"

Unless she'd taken a stupid pill since he'd last seen her, she knew damn well what he was suggesting. And since he wasn't about to play games, he said, "I just want to be sure you're living up to your end of our deal. That you didn't decide a contract killer was simply too good a story to sit on for even a day or two and—"

"You really have a nerve," she snapped.

"Is that a no? You're saying you haven't sent anything to the *Post?*"

"Of course I haven't. And what is your problem, Dan? I mean I can understand that you didn't trust me when I was a complete stranger. But after your own Lydia—whoever she is—checked me out and told you I was—"

"How the hell do you know about Lydia?"

"I was kind of listening when you called her."

"*Kind of listening?* Even though I phoned her from Billy's library? With the door closed?"

"I have excellent hearing."

"Yeah, I'll bet you do. Especially when your ear's pressed against a door."

"I'm a journalist. People aren't always forthright with us so we have to do whatever."

He gave her a black look.

She completely ignored it, adding, "And I was standing right beside you when Lydia called back."

"How did you know it was her?"

"Oh, for heaven's sake. How could I not? Your body language totally gave you away. At any rate, it was obvious that she had only good things to say about me."

"There's a difference between good things and not bad things," he muttered.

"Whatever. You wouldn't have let me come with you if she'd said anything even marginally bad. So why you'd be suspicious enough to think I might—"

"Okay, okay. I get the point. You kept your word. Now tell me why you took such a circuitous route that you were over an hour getting back here."

"Ah. Well."

"Ah, well, what?"

She suddenly looked uncomfortable enough to make him edgy.

"I have something to show you," she said.

From that moment on, Mickey seemed to be moving at a snail's pace, although he suspected the problem was his own impatience. Whatever she had to show him, however, required her to first get her laptop set up on the desk, then connect her camera to the computer with a length of cable.

"This won't take much longer," she said, once she appeared to have things organized. I'm just going to download a picture."

"It's a digital camera?" he asked.

"Uh-huh."

"I hadn't realized that," he said, watching her key a command into the computer. "All the others I've seen have been little."

"Well, professional quality digitals are still awfully expensive, so it's mostly just serious photographers who have them. But they do look more like old-fashioned cameras than the cheaper ones. And, really, for all intents and purposes, the only difference is the memory disk cards instead of film."

"Plus the little screen on the back," he pointed out.

"Uh-huh. And the fact that you can make mini-movies with them."

"But aside from those minor details," he said dryly, "this is exactly the same as an old-fashioned camera."

Mickey gave him a look that said there was no need for him to be a smart-ass, then she focused on the laptop's screen as a photo of a man appeared.

In his late twenties or early thirties, he was rather nondescript looking, with medium dark brown hair and eyes and no particularly distinguishing features.

The sort who, unless you knew him, you'd never notice in a crowd.

While Dan gazed at the picture, Mickey said, "That's our contract killer."

It took a second for her words to sink in.

Once they had, he caught her gaze and said, "You aren't serious."

"Yes, I am. That's him."

He looked at the screen again, thinking the man's wouldn't-stand-out-in-a-crowd appearance was perfect for what he did. Witnesses who only saw him briefly would be hard-pressed to give the cops a helpful description.

Mickey had seen him for more than "briefly," though. She'd seen him long enough to take a picture.

He could feel a stirring of panic in his chest—and he never panicked.

The entire time he'd been waiting for her to show up, and wondering where the hell she was, he'd been afraid that she'd done something crazy. And sure enough, she had.

Even his wildest imaginings hadn't been quite this crazy, however. And despite the fact that half of him was downright thrilled to have the picture, the other half was appalled that she'd snapped it.

After warning himself to speak calmly, because if she realized the full magnitude of her mistake *she'd* be the one in panic mode, he said, "Since he's looking directly at the camera, he must have seen you take the shot."

She nodded, her expression sheepish. "Which explains the circuitous route."

His heartbeat revved up to double time. "Let me be sure I've got things straight," he said. "There's no doubt at all that he knows you took this."

"No. And actually, I took several. This is a good, clear one, though."

Not picture but pictures. Plural.

He knew he shouldn't utter another word. There was no undoing what she'd done. Yet the next thing he knew he was saying, "So you just stood there and—"

"Dan, we have pictures of him. We're not dealing with a complete mystery man anymore."

"Right. You're right. Having pictures is fantastic. Except for the fact that he knows you've got them. And that he'll want to kill you before you can do anything with them!"

Oh, hell. So much for not putting her into panic mode. He just wasn't good at dealing with amateurs.

She paled a little, but she said simply, "Well, I'd already figured that out. But snapping them was an automatic reaction. I spotted him staring at me and just knew who he was and… Dan, I had the camera in my hand and I didn't think. *Literally,* I didn't consciously think about what I was doing. One second I was simply staring back at him and the next I was clicking away."

"Jeez, Mickey. It's a wonder he didn't kill you right then and there."

Oh, hell, he'd done it again.

"I ran."

"You mean he pulled his gun but you—"

"Well, he started to. But before he got it out I took off. And I didn't stop running until I had such a pain in my side that I had to."

"Oh, man. Man, oh, man."

"It's not as bad as it seems."

"Oh?"

He stood gazing at her, waiting to hear why she thought that being on a contract killer's hit list—undoubtedly only one name beneath Billy's—wasn't just about the worst thing in the world.

"He has no idea who I am," she said. "Or where I am."

"You're sure he didn't follow you?"

"Positive."

"Absolutely?"

She nodded. "I kept looking back. I'd have seen him."

Maybe she would have, but not if the guy was good enough.

And he probably was, given that he was a pro.

"Wait here," he said. "Lock the door when I leave and don't open it to anyone except me."

"But—"

"Just do it," he ordered, stepping out into the empty hallway.

CHAPTER EIGHT

TURK SAT in the hotel's lobby, hidden behind a copy of the *Wall Street Journal* that someone had left behind, assuring himself everything was under control.

Of course, this damn job should already be over and done with. But sometimes shit happened and you just had to cope with it. And that was exactly what he'd been doing since things had gone wrong at NBS.

Even his car, which he'd left parked near the studio when he'd taken off after the woman, was now just down the street waiting for him—thanks to Louie, who'd gone and collected it.

Louie was a useful guy to know. Always only a phone call away and willing to do pretty much anything as long as the price was right.

Of course, with most people it was just a matter of how much. He didn't need to look farther than across the lobby to see an example of that.

The desk clerk's going rate was a hundred bucks, and for that he'd been happy to check through the registration cards, which was how Turk knew that his problems, currently sitting up in Room 803, were a Mr. and Mrs. Daniel O'Neill of Hartford, Connecticut.

At least that was how they'd registered.

But whether those were their real names or not, the question of the moment was how long he'd have to wait before one, or both of them, came downstairs.

He had to pee something fierce, but he didn't want to move from where he was.

As soon as he did, something would happen. It was Murphy's Law. Well, maybe it wasn't Murphy's, but definitely somebody's.

Trying not to think about how loudly nature was calling, he let the name Hartford ramble around in the trivia section of his mind.

Hartford. The state capital. Known as Insurance City because so many insurance companies had their headquarters there.

However, he'd bet Mr. and Mrs. Daniel O'Neill had nothing to do with insurance.

Their business was with Billy Brent, and he just wished he could figure out precisely what their game was.

Yesterday, after encountering Daniel at Billy's retreat, he hadn't been quite sure whether O'Neill was some sort of bodyguard or merely a decoy. But given the way he'd acted outside NBS, the guy had to be a bodyguard.

How did *Mrs.* O'Neill fit in, though? What kind of bodyguard brought his wife along on a job?

He just didn't know. But his laptop was stashed under the front seat of his car, so as soon as he had the chance he'd see what he could find out about the two of them.

For the moment, though, he had to hang in here and wait for whatever happened next.

Wondering again how long his problems would be upstairs, he looked back over toward the desk.

After he'd parted with more money, the clerk had recalled Daniel coming in about an hour ago with a second man, one who'd been intent on keeping his face hidden. Then, another hundred had helped the guy remember that the unidentified man had left, not long ago, with a third fellow.

Obviously it was Billy Brent who'd been and gone.

But who had the third man been?

And where had he taken Billy?

That one didn't require much guessing. They'd gone someplace where they figured Billy would be safe from *him.* As for exactly where, he'd eventually find out. And maybe eventually wouldn't be long in coming.

With any luck, the O'Neills planned to meet up with Billy later, and if they did, he'd be tagging along.

From where he was sitting, he could just see the doorway to the stairwell. And the elevators were in plain sight, so there was no way he'd miss anyone leaving.

He glanced in the direction of the stairs once more, then looked at the indicators to see if either car was on its way down.

Neither was, but Daniel and the missus weren't going to stay put forever.

As Turk raised the newspaper back to eyelevel, his thoughts returned to that screwup outside NBS.

The O'Neill woman was one of the last people on earth he'd have expected to see in New York.

There she'd been, though. With a camera this time, instead of a gun. And she'd known who he was. He'd seen the way she'd looked at him and there wasn't any doubt.

Maybe she was psychic. Or she had X-ray vision that had let her see through his mask yesterday.

But regardless of what unusual talents she might possess, every time he thought about what had happened he felt angry again. Both at her and at himself—for being so careless.

He'd been totally concentrating on that limo, feeling in-the-bones-sure that within moments Billy Brent was going to emerge and the job would be over.

Then, out of nowhere, O'Neill had suddenly been in charge. And an instant later the stretch was speeding away.

He'd been so taken aback that he'd stepped from behind his cover without thinking. And that was when he'd spotted her.

She'd been even more of a shocker than her husband. Enough of one that he'd momentarily frozen.

The next thing he knew she'd had her camera aimed at him and… His heart was racing just from the recollection, so he told himself to chill.

Maybe he had screwed up, but he was back on track now. And the good news was that he hadn't been freaked enough to go with his first instinct and simply take her out. He'd gotten as far as reaching for his gun, then had realized he was courting disaster.

One clean shot at Billy, from behind a pillar, and he'd have been gone before anyone even figured out where the shot had come from.

But the whole point of killing the woman, right then and there, would have been to grab her camera. And he'd have put himself in plain view while he was getting it.

It was just a good thing he'd realized how stupid the idea was before he'd acted on it. Because if he had, some idiot could easily have tackled him.

At the very least, half the suits on the street would have been hitting 911 on their cell phones.

There were neighborhoods in this city where people often "didn't notice" shootings. But they hardly included the NBS block of Fifth Avenue.

That meant the entire area would have been swarming with cops in no time. And even if he'd gotten away, he'd have felt like such an amateur that he'd have started doubting himself. Which would not have been good.

When you played in the majors, self-confidence was everything.

He took a slow in-and-out breath, still not quite able to believe that he'd considered whacking her with a hundred people watching.

Oh, not that he'd ruled out the idea of killing her. Loose ends were always bad news, so he'd eventually eliminate both her *and* Daniel.

But this morning had been neither the right time nor the right place. It was a good thing he'd realized that and had handled things the way he should have—had waited to see what she'd do and followed her when she'd taken off.

After that, things had begun looking up.

Despite her roundabout route, he hadn't lost track of the woman on the way here. And he was sure she had no idea that he'd tailed her. She hadn't even glanced back until she'd covered the first couple of blocks. Then, the few times she *had* checked over her shoulder, she hadn't seen him.

He knew how to follow someone without being spotted. In his profession, that was an important skill.

The only real bad news was he hadn't gotten that camera.

Dammit, he should never have let the bitch see him, let alone capture him on film. Or maybe it wasn't film. Maybe she'd been using one of those digital jobs.

Shit. His love of modern technology didn't extend to cameras. Photography just wasn't his thing.

He hadn't taken a picture in years, and when it came to digitals he knew almost nothing. But what little he did know was enough to make him sweat, because if her camera *was* a digital, she could have made prints of those pictures by now. Or sent them to anyone in the world.

Like to the cops, for example.

He carefully considered that possibility once again and came to the same conclusion as he had earlier. The problem wasn't nearly as serious as it could be.

He planned his jobs so carefully that he'd never been arrested, let alone charged. Not as an adult, at least. And thanks to the country's bleeding-heart liberals, his juvie records were sealed. So even if the cops ran whatever pictures she had they wouldn't find a match.

Besides, could she really say anything about him that would raise their interest?

He didn't see how.

All she could tell them was that she *thought* the man she'd photographed had been waiting outside NBS to kill Billy Brent. And that she *thought* he was the same guy who'd shown up at Billy's place—on the other side of the continent—yesterday.

Only she'd have to admit that she couldn't be sure about that because yesterday's guy had been wearing a mask.

It wasn't a story the police would take seriously, pictures or no pictures. So he just had to stop worrying about the damn things.

Otherwise, he was going to send his blood pressure into the stratosphere.

EVEN THOUGH THEIR ROOM was on the eighth floor, Dan had taken the stairs, partly because stairwells made good hiding places and partly because there were floor indicators above the elevators on one.

If the hit man was lurking even closer than out on the street, giving him advance warning would be defeating the purpose of the exercise.

When he reached the lobby, there was no one in sight except the desk clerk, who was a younger and even more bored looking fellow than last night's.

Quickly, Dan strode across to the entrance door and walked a few feet out onto the sidewalk, far enough to let him see up and down the block.

He spotted nothing suspicious, although that hardly guaranteed there was no one watching the hotel. But he didn't want to waste time doing a more thorough look-see while Mickey was alone upstairs.

After going back into the lobby, he looked into the men's room. It proved empty, so he headed up to the eighth floor again, only too aware that the sort of rudimentary check he'd just done was as good as useless. And that he couldn't let his guard down, not even a little, simply because there'd been no sign of their killer.

The issue, here, wasn't the fact that he hadn't seen the guy, or that Mickey didn't believe he'd followed her. It was whether or not a hit man would have decided that going after her was his best move.

Dan tried to put himself in the other man's place, hardly easy when he didn't know him. But if *he'd* been the one waiting outside NBS to shoot Billy, and *his* plan had blown up in his face…

Well, his first problem would have been trying to figure out exactly what Mickey would do.

When she took off, he wouldn't have known

whether she was merely running to get away or if she was calling the cops as she ran—to tell them her location and that an armed man was chasing her.

With her long hair, and all the stuff she'd been toting, she could easily have been using a phone without anyone behind her being able to see it.

Given that, their guy might have decided to just play things safe and put as much distance between them as he could. Yes. That was certainly one possibility.

On the other hand, as he'd told Mickey only a few minutes ago, a contract killer would be damn concerned about someone snapping his picture. And if he figured he might be able to prevent her from doing anything with the shots, he'd try.

Hell, it was a complete toss-up. There was no way of being sure what the guy had done. And just because there didn't seem to be anyone keeping the hotel under surveillance…

But he'd already been there. And when his thoughts began running in circles it was time to shift gears. So for the time being he'd stop worrying about *where* the killer was and focus on *who* he was.

Those pictures Mickey had would give them a good chance of establishing that. And even contract killers lived someplace, so if they could actually learn his identity…

Dan reached Room 803 and knocked on the door, quietly identifying himself.

"See any trace of our friend?" Mickey asked as soon as he stepped inside.

When he shook his head, she looked distinctly relieved.

''What have you been doing?'' he asked, glancing at her computer and seeing print on the screen rather than the picture.

''Working on my story. I figure that if I basically write it as we go, then I'll only have to add the ending and edit it when...well, when we get to the end. In the meantime,'' she added, ''what do we do with my photo of our killer? Give a copy to the police?''

''No.''

''Really? But what about all those computer records they have? The centralized ones that cover the whole country? If he's ever been arrested, shouldn't the cops be able to tell you who he is?''

''Well, yeah, they might be able to. But only if he *has* been arrested.''

''Isn't it worth checking, though? I mean, if your company has all those arrangements you were telling me about, the police would be cooperative, wouldn't they?''

He shrugged. ''Probably. But once we told the NYPD what was going on...assuming they took us seriously, they'd start looking for him. And that would only scare him into hiding.''

''He'd know?''

''Yeah, he'd know. Not all cops are good at keeping their mouths shut. Some are even eager to talk, as long as they get paid for it.''

''But if he did go into hiding, he wouldn't be after Billy, so—''

"That would only be temporary. At any rate, I have far more faith in Risk Control International than I do in the police. So what we'll do is send a copy of the picture to Lydia. Get her working on identifying him. And it wouldn't be a bad idea to e-mail a copy to yourself, too," he added, not really sure he should.

He figured Mickey was a whole lot more frightened than she was letting on, and he hated to scare her even more. But it *wouldn't* be a bad idea.

After eyeing him for a moment, she said, "You mean e-mail it with a message saying that, if I end up dead, this is a picture of the guy who probably killed me?"

"Well, it couldn't hurt."

She stared silently at the floor, then finally looked at him again and said, "You never did tell me who Lydia is."

He was glad that she'd changed the subject. Talking about the possibility of her getting killed would do nothing even remotely positive for her mental health.

Or his, for that matter.

"Lydia's a research operative at RCI," he explained. "If our guy's got a record, she'll find it."

"She can access police files?"

"If he's got a record, she'll find it," he repeated.

Maybe Mickey had turned out to be trustworthy, but he'd probably already told her more about the company than he should have.

And he'd never admit to any journalist that RCI

people simply did what needed doing—without many qualms about exactly how they did it.

"Why don't I call her right now," he said. "And while I'm telling her what the story is, you can e-mail her the picture."

MICKEY HADN'T BLINKED TWICE while e-mailing their hit man's picture to Lydia, but sending it to herself had given her a *really* creepy-crawly feeling.

After it had gone, she wandered across the room and sank into one of the tub chairs, suddenly exhausted.

Even though she kept in good shape, running as far and fast as she had from NBS had been more exercise than she normally got in a single dose.

She took off her sneakers, wiggled her toes, then looked over at Dan.

He was standing in the far corner, facing the wall and quietly talking to Lydia on his cellular, obviously trying to prevent any eavesdropping this time. But he didn't really have to worry about that.

Since she'd been too involved with what she was doing to listen in on the first part of his conversation, there wasn't much point in tuning in now, when it had to be almost over.

Besides, she already knew the basics of what he was saying, so she just let her thoughts drift, and they ended up at the moment when she'd finally made it back here to the hotel room.

She'd knocked on the door, Dan had opened it,

and his relieved expression had literally taken her breath away.

It had also given her the message that her initial impression of him needed revision. Obviously, he had more emotional depth than was initially apparent.

Dan O'Neill wasn't only concerned about himself and his clients after all; he had the capacity to care about other people.

About her.

That realization had started her heart doing a funny little dance.

Oh, she knew his greeting had only consisted of a gruff "Where the hell have you been?"

And maybe he'd just admitted to being "a little concerned" about her. But she'd known it was more than a little, which had made her feel warm and bubbly inside.

Of course, she wasn't sure that was at all good.

Well, to be entirely truthful, she was pretty sure it wasn't even slightly good. She certainly hadn't forgotten that the man was *anything* but her type.

From what she could tell, they didn't have a single thing in common. However, to say that some sort of connection had developed between them would be another in the series of understatements they kept adding to. And the connection was more than just a simple sexual attraction.

Not that she'd try to deny there was a major physical component. She also wouldn't try to deny that Daniel O'Neill was growing on her as a person.

She'd come to see he wasn't entirely lacking in positive attributes. He was intelligent. And honest. And his dry sense of humor reminded her of her brothers.

Little else about him did, though. And his lifestyle was so completely different from most men's....

Besides, she'd never want to get involved with someone who, even if he did have more emotions than she'd initially thought, kept them so tightly locked away that they might as well not exist.

Of course, she couldn't forget that he hadn't given her any indication he *wanted* to get involved, which probably made the subject of how he handled his emotions irrelevant.

And even if it wasn't, reality hadn't changed. He was still so far removed from Mr. Right that he might as well be a different species.

What had she decided her mother would say about him?

He was the sort of man she should run, not walk, away from. That was it. The sort of man nobody in her right mind would consider good husband and father material.

Lord, a man who was constantly on the move, working wherever his jobs took him, couldn't even be considered good dating material.

"Uh-huh, sure," he said into the phone.

She looked at him as he added, "Anything at all that you can find."

Then, while he listened to whatever Lydia was saying, he glanced across the room, caught her eye and smiled.

When that was enough to send a rush of liquid heat through her, she realized she could be in real trouble.

TURK WAS BREATHING more easily again, but it had taken him a few minutes to get his heartbeat out of overdrive.

O'Neill's coming downstairs had been a very close call. And if Lady Luck hadn't been on the right side… But she had been, which was all that mattered.

Besides, he hadn't actually slipped up. He'd simply succumbed to the call of nature.

The longer he'd waited in the lobby, the more desperately he'd needed to use the john—until he'd finally had no choice but to risk a minute away from his post. And it was when he'd been coming back from the men's room that he'd spotted O'Neill.

That had sure thrown him for a few seconds. But he'd done the sensible thing and stayed right where he was while the guy checked the street.

Then, when he'd begun to retrace his steps, the old gut instincts had kicked in, warning him not to retreat back into the men's room.

Instead, he'd ducked into the ladies' room, and that had turned out to be a good move. With the door cracked open an inch, he'd been able to watch as O'Neill checked the other washroom.

Fortunately, he'd left it at that and gone upstairs again. Now it was just a matter of waiting until he came down once more.

The question was, would his wife be with him?

If so, there'd be only one thing to do. Follow them and hope they led him to Billy. But if O'Neill came down alone, it would be decision time.

He'd either have to trail after him or make a trip upstairs and have a little talk with wifey about her pictures.

CHAPTER NINE

DAN FINISHED his conversation and set down the phone, but didn't immediately turn toward Mickey.

He could feel her eyes on him, and knew that as soon as he looked her way she'd start asking about what Lydia had said. Or what they were going to do next.

And since *they* weren't going to be doing anything next, he needed time to organize his thoughts.

The situation was far more dangerous than it had been before Mickey had taken those pictures, and he had to convince her to go home.

The problem was, given her stubborn nature, he didn't have much hope of her agreeing to leave without an argument.

She might be frightened, but he wasn't sure that she was frightened enough. Hell, he wasn't sure about a whole lot of things, because his thoughts were nowhere near organized.

Twenty minutes ago, he'd been trying to watch what he said so she wouldn't get too scared.

Now he'd decided there was no such thing as her being too scared. Not if it meant she'd peacefully agree to leave. So what he had to do was make sure that she recognized exactly how much higher she'd raised the risk factor.

As long as he did that, and made it perfectly clear that heading back to San Francisco wouldn't mean forfeiting her damn exclusive… Right, that was the key.

If she suspected there was any chance of missing out, he'd have a far harder time convincing her. But as long as she understood the only change in the game plan was that she couldn't stay here with him for the duration…

After a few seconds devoted exclusively to psyching himself up, he glanced over to where she was sitting.

"So?" she said the instant he caught her gaze. "Where do we go from here?"

Knowing he couldn't delay the inevitable any longer, he crossed the room and moved the other chair around so he could sit facing her.

It took him about two heartbeats to realize he should have stayed where he was.

He'd have been far better off keeping his distance than getting close enough that his knees were almost touching hers. And close enough that he could smell her jasmine-and-four-o'clocks scent.

"So?" she prompted again, while he was still searching for a good way to begin.

Since he hadn't quite found the words he wanted, he stalled by saying, "Well, unless Lydia comes up with a name and address—or at the very minimum, a name—I can forget about the possibility of just nailing the killer and forcing him to tell me who hired him.''

Mickey nodded, then said, ''You know, I've asked you before how you'd make him talk.''

When he just let that lie in the air between them, she added, ''But you still haven't told me.''

''No, I guess I haven't.''

And he had no intention of getting into it now. So, instead, in an eminently reasonable tone, he said, ''Look, there's something more important we need to discuss.''

She nodded, then waited for him to elaborate. ''I realize you don't think our guy followed you,'' he said, ''but the odds that he did are about ninety-nine percent.''

''Oh?'' She studied him suspiciously. ''Then why didn't you see him when you went downstairs?''

''Because I only did a cursory check. And because he's a pro. I doubt going down there was worth my while,'' he added when she didn't look even marginally less suspicious. ''And right this minute,'' he pressed on, ''he's probably standing across the street waiting for us to come out—spending the down time thinking about how he's going to get his hands on your camera.''

He hesitated, then reminded himself he had to be as tough as he could on her and added, ''And the easiest way of getting it would be to kill you.''

Without saying a word, she pushed herself up from her chair and walked over to the window.

"No one's watching the hotel," she said, turning toward him again after looking out for a few seconds.

"No one you can see."

She shrugged. "Even if he was there, he'd know that I've had more than enough time to do whatever I wanted with those shots."

Dan watched her head back across the room. When she sat down again, she shifted her chair an inch or two closer to his, which was all it took to make him even more intensely aware of her nearness—and make him feel as if a ball of heat had suddenly begun burning inside his chest.

He tried to convince himself the sensation was merely his frustration level rising, and did his best to force it lower before saying, "Mickey, he might know you've had time to do something with the pictures, but he'll be hoping you haven't done anything yet. And hoping he can get at them before you do. Which means it isn't safe for you to be in New York any longer. Not that it ever was," he continued quickly. "But now it's a lot *less* safe.

"And before you start into mathematical probabilities again," he added before she could speak, "let's get something else straight. We're well beyond the fact that not many journalists get killed while they're on assignment. We're at the fact that this particular killer has good reason to come after you. So the only sensible option is for you to go back to San Francisco until I've sorted things out. As soon as I have, I'll give you every detail you want for your story."

"Dan, that—"

"I'm not reneging on our deal. I'm only saying your life's in serious danger. And that getting yourself killed is too high a price to pay for *anything.* Even for a front-page byline."

He forced a smile on the premise that a little humor could hardly hurt. However, in this instance it apparently wasn't going to help, either.

She didn't smile back. And while he wouldn't exactly call the look she was giving him a glare, he couldn't think of any other word to describe it.

"The odds that he followed me are ninety-nine percent, huh?" she said at last. "There's no chance you just pulled that figure out of the air, is there?"

"Look, all I'm—"

"If he'd followed me, I'd have seen him. I told you that before."

"Mickey, he's a professional hit man. How many people do you think he'd manage to kill if they spotted him following them?"

"There's no need to be sarcastic."

"I'm not being sarcastic. I'm just saying I don't want you ending up dead."

"I have no intention of ending up dead!"

"Good. I'm glad. And the best way to prevent that from happening is by getting the hell out of New York. As I specifically remember telling you before, keeping Billy alive and learning who wants him eliminated is *my* job, not yours."

"But getting the exclusive as this story plays out is *my* job! You heard me on the phone with my editor. I practically begged him to let me come here with you. And I guaranteed him that I'd deliver. Guaranteed both him *and* the editor in chief. They put their faith in me. And my expense report is already going to be sky-high. So if I let them down... Dan, I just *have* to cover the story firsthand. Be right here while it unfolds. That's what you and I agreed to. And it's what I promised the *Post* I'd do."

"Now wait a minute. I don't think that's quite what you and I agreed to. I think—"

"You know, you don't have a very good memory for details. But let's not argue," she added before he could say that he had an excellent memory for details.

"I haven't been any hindrance to you so far, have I?" she pressed on.

"Well..."

"Exactly. I've been a help."

"Mickey, I don't think I'd quite say—"

"I probably kept you from getting killed at Billy's place. Remember?"

"Yes, of course I remember. But that was then and this is—"

"And I might do it again today. Or tomorrow. Don't forget about the old two-heads-are-better-than-one rule. And the one that says four eyes are better than two."

"That is *not* a rule. You just made it up," he pointed out, realizing, as he spoke, that he sounded frighteningly like a four-year-old.

"Dan, I—"

"Mickey, give it a rest," he said, carefully speaking in a distinctly adult tone. "I've had it with your manipulating me into doing things I don't want to do. Totally had it. No, that didn't come out right. What I meant is that I've had it with your manipulating me into letting *you* do things I don't want you to do."

"Manipulating isn't a very nice word," she said quietly.

"If the shoe fits," the four-year-old's voice muttered.

She hesitated, then said, "Dan, I know I sometimes seem pushy. But, growing up with three older brothers, I had to learn to stand up for my rights or I wouldn't have had any. So...look, I'm really sorry that we see this situation differently, but if I don't—"

"No," he interrupted. "No more discussion. We've reached the end of the line. We're going to phone and book you a flight to San Francisco. On the first plane with an empty seat."

Mickey said nothing more, just sat gazing at him, and for a moment he actually thought he'd won.

He should have known better.

After she eyed him for another few seconds, she said, "Dan, I am *not* going home. I realize I can't force you to let me tag along with you, but..."

When she ended that sentence with a shrug, he could feel his blood beginning to boil.

This was precisely the same trick she'd pulled earlier when she'd told him that if he didn't want her to go to NBS with him she'd go by herself.

But what did she think she'd do this time? Wander around Manhattan, by herself, looking for a killer she could now put a face to?

Well, she wouldn't have to look very bloody hard. Odds were their guy would be right behind her. With his gun drawn.

Man, oh, man. There wasn't the slightest doubt that Mickey Westover was the most infuriating woman he'd ever met.

In fact, if someone told him she was the most infuriating woman in the entire world, he wouldn't be even mildly surprised. Actually, he'd be more than willing to believe that she was the most in the entire universe.

She knew she had him. Knew he wouldn't cut her loose when he figured their hit man would dearly love to kill her.

Hell, he half wanted to kill her himself. Half wanted to kill her and half wanted to kiss her.

That thought jumped out to ambush him from nowhere. And even though he did his best to ignore it, he couldn't. Not when he was looking directly at her lush mouth.

He tried to force his eyes away from it, but he couldn't do that, either.

"Dan?" she said softly.

He swallowed hard, certain that just watching the way her lips moved when she said his name could drive him crazy in no time.

"What?" he managed.

"I know you're only thinking about what's best for me, and I appreciate that. I honestly do. But you're thinking about it from *your* perspective. And, really, since it's me we're talking about, I'm the only one who can decide what's best."

"Mickey, getting killed isn't best from *anybody's* perspective. And I can't—"

"No, wait. Just listen to me for a minute, okay?"

He made himself nod.

After all, he had started out determined to be perfectly reasonable. And he *did* know it was the only approach that had any chance of working.

She took a deep breath, then said, "I'm sure I've already more than belabored the fact that this story is terribly important to me—that it can make my career."

Or make you a corpse, he wanted to say, but he succeeded in keeping his mouth shut.

"So let's think about it from another angle," she continued. "You're a specialist. An expert in personal security. Shouldn't I be safe with you?"

Uh-oh, he didn't like where she was going with that question. And he certainly wasn't about to let her manipulate him yet again.

"Safe with me," he said. "But aren't you the woman who told me you don't need baby-sitting?"

"I don't. You've seen that for yourself. I'm only saying that I wouldn't be in nearly as much danger as you're trying to make out because I'd be with you. But regardless of that, I haven't been in your way so far and I'm not going to be. And don't forget that if I wasn't here we wouldn't have a picture of our killer, which might turn out to be exactly the advantage we need.

"For all we know, Lydia will call any minute to let you know who he is. And where he lives. Then you'll still have a chance to just make him tell you who's behind the contract."

Before he could formulate a response to that, Mickey said, "I want to ask you something."

"What?"

"Have you ever let anyone get killed? Someone you were protecting, I mean?"

"That has absolutely nothing to do with this. I—"

"Dan, it has everything to do with this. So tell me the truth. You've never let a soul you had any responsibility for get killed, have you?"

"Well, no, but—"

"Then I rest my case."

He exhaled slowly, tempted to point out that he didn't have any responsibility for her. But why bother when, like it or not, he *felt* responsible?

Hell, he might as well just give in right here and now.

Better yet, he should have saved himself a whole lot of aggravation and given in as soon as she'd said she wasn't going home.

ONCE DAN HAD FALLEN SILENT, Mickey pushed herself up from her chair and wandered over to the window again, trying to look casual but feeling tense.

Just nervous energy, she told herself, and didn't like it when an imaginary voice whispered, *Just nervous energy and fear.*

Her gaze drifted along the street below, then her blood froze as she spotted a man standing on the far side.

He was leaning against the driver's door of one of the vehicles in the row of parked cars and gazing over at the hotel.

From eight stories up, she could only see the top of his head, not his face, but he looked to be of medium height and build. And the lightweight beige jacket slung over his shoulder could easily be the one the hit man had been wearing earlier.

As her heartbeat started to race, a woman appeared beneath the window and hurried across to him.

When they gave each other a quick hug before climbing into the car, Mickey could feel her heart rate beginning to return to normal.

Still, she knew, deep down, that Dan was right. A professional killer could have followed her here without her realizing it. Her powers of observation wouldn't have been at their best while she was running for her life.

Staring out at nothing after the car drove away, she tried hard to focus her thoughts on the key issue, which was, of course, that she'd apparently won the argument about staying.

Dan hadn't called her bluff. And that was most fortunate, considering she didn't know what she'd have done if he had.

No, that wasn't true. She did know. She just didn't want to think about how close she'd come to being forced to go home.

But he could easily have told her that if she stayed in New York she'd be on her own. And that would have been the end of her scoop.

Without him, she wouldn't have the full story about Billy Brent. No access to it, at least. She'd also have had no choice about heading back to San Francisco.

Although she'd never admit it aloud, she realized that she'd be totally insane to remain in New York, on her own, with a killer itching to get at her.

She might be ambitious, but she didn't have a death wish. So she was immensely relieved that Dan hadn't shown her the door.

However, the fact she'd convinced him to give in had her feeling so guilty that her focus was slip-sliding all over the place.

If he'd said that he wanted her to go home because she was in his way, or had given her any of a hundred other different bogus excuses, she'd simply have been angry.

But his reason was that he was worried about her safety.

And she didn't suspect him of lying. While they were arguing, she'd seen the truth in his eyes.

They hadn't been their usual color of cold blue steel. Rather, they'd been dark with emotion, which had made her feel…

Lord, that was something she was afraid to seriously contemplate. But at the very minimum, she was feeling far differently toward Daniel O'Neill than she had in the beginning.

How could she not be when the things she liked about the man just kept piling up?

Oh, she hadn't begun thinking he'd be anyone's idea of Mr. Perfect. Her mind hadn't turned to utter mush.

Still, no matter how often she told herself she shouldn't even consider getting involved with him, every time she caught him watching her she practically melted.

The problem, of course, was his damn animal magnetism.

No, the *real* problem was that the more time she spent with him the stronger it was growing.

Or maybe the trouble lay with her.

Maybe the strength of his magnetism hadn't changed one bit, but she was becoming more and more aware of it. Or less and less immune to it.

Regardless of how that process worked, if things continued the way they'd been going, in another day or two she'd be so aware of it she wouldn't be able to function.

And that made the problem extremely critical, especially when he wasn't the sort of man her brain wanted her to have anything to do with. Anything aside from the Billy Brent story, that was.

Unfortunately, it was clear that her brain wasn't in complete control of the situation.

Complete?

She considered that for a second and decided it probably wasn't even in marginal control.

"Mickey?"

Turning from the window, she looked over at Dan.

A mere glance at his expression told her his anger had dissipated, which was just something else that had her feeling more positively toward him.

The man didn't hold grudges.

He might have been mad as hell at her a couple of minutes ago, but he'd apparently already come to terms with the fact that she was staying.

And it had been the same story earlier.

He'd been bound and determined that she wasn't going to NBS with him. And he'd been furious when she'd held her ground. Yet once they'd arrived there he'd simply accepted that she was along and proceeded accordingly.

She certainly had to give him credit for being flexible. Which was a lucky thing for her.

A lot of other men would…

But he wasn't a lot of other men. He was…

She tried to keep the word *special* from forming in her mind, but couldn't quite manage to. Then she tried to look away from him, but couldn't quite do that, either.

The longer he held her gaze, the stronger that melting sensation inside her felt, until she was at serious risk that either her legs would give out on her or she'd dissolve into a puddle on the floor.

"If you're staying," he said at last, "there are some things we have to talk about."

CHAPTER TEN

MICKEY STARTED BACK across the hotel room toward Dan, uneasily aware that even though she'd broken eye contact, he was still watching her.

She asked herself who else he'd be watching when there were only the two of them in the room, but trying to make light of the situation did no good. Not when a mere glance confirmed that she hadn't been misreading the *way* he was watching her.

If she'd had any lingering doubts as to whether he felt the pull between them as powerfully as she did, they'd have been banished by now. His eyes were *that* hungry.

She absently licked her lips, immediately realizing she shouldn't have. She shouldn't do anything that could be construed as even remotely provocative when the look-but-don't-touch tension between them was already practically sizzling.

If she could turn back time and prevent it from developing, she would. Since she wasn't a magician, however, she'd just have to be very aware and very careful.

Because she absolutely, positively, didn't want this thing—for lack of a better word—going any further.

Absolutely? Positively?

Mentally shaking her head, she asked herself who she was trying to kid.

Maybe her brain was saying this *thing* was bad news. But if she added the way her pulse was racing to the fact that her insides were on fire, she got an entirely different message.

Yet how could this possibly be happening? How could she be growing practically obsessed with a man she knew was wrong for her?

Especially here and now? When not only was she after the story of her life, but there might well be a hit man watching the hotel just waiting for his chance to kill her?

Lord, she had to get her head back on straight. And make her hormones stop dancing the tarantella.

Right. That was the way to handle this. She'd simply force herself to quit practically drooling over Daniel O'Neill and concentrate on the important issues.

Reaching the chair, she sat down facing him again, hoping she didn't look as hot as she felt.

Then she silently began repeating a mantra of *focus, focus, focus,* while he said, "We could be in New York for a while."

She had no idea whether by "for a while" he was thinking a couple of days or weeks, but since she intended to hang in for however long the duration was, she simply said, "And what, exactly, will we be doing?"

"Well, remember I told you that Billy and I discussed who might want him dead badly enough to hire a hit man?''

''Uh-huh. You said the list was endless.''

''Did I?'' He smiled, which was all it took to make her feel even hotter.

As he added, ''That was pretty indiscreet of me,'' she told herself to be grateful it hadn't been a full-blown smile. One of those might have made her ignite.

''Indiscreet,'' she repeated, her mind snagging that word to concentrate on. ''Yes...well...I guess you were overtired.''

''That must have been it. At any rate, the list of really likely suspects isn't all that extensive. It's just that, in addition to the likelies, there are a lot of...long shots, I guess we could call them.''

When he paused, she said, ''I have a question. When I first asked if you thought it was a professional killer after Billy, you said *probably.* Have we gone from probably to definitely?''

''Yeah. I wasn't entirely sure before he put in his appearance at Billy's. But after our exchange there, I didn't have any doubt.''

''Why not?''

Dan shrugged. ''Just for starters, an amateur wouldn't have traveled all that way for a shot at Billy. He'd have picked a more convenient place. And a big Magnum is a pro's gun. Then there was the way he snuck up on us and...well, everything just added up to a contract hit.''

"But before that you had some doubt because…?"

"Because a crazy fan has been stalking Billy for the past six or seven months. And a stalker who escalates to killing generally tries to do the job himself. So I wasn't entirely sure I was dealing with a pro until I saw our guy in action. But getting back to who hired him—most of the people Billy figures might want him dead are right here in Manhattan."

"Really?"

"You were thinking L.A.?"

She nodded.

"Well, don't forget he spent years on Broadway. And that he's still in New York fairly often. There *is* one other serious suspect in California, though. Aside from the stalker."

When she eyed him, waiting for him to continue, his not-sure-he-could-fully-trust-her expression appeared, shooting a sharp dart of annoyance into her.

Maybe she had come to see that he possessed some admirable qualities, but he was just too darned suspicious for her taste. She didn't want a relationship that wasn't based on trust.

Firmly, she reminded herself that she didn't want a relationship, period. Not with Daniel O'Neill. It was only her hormones that were misinformed on that count.

She turned her full attention back to him as he began speaking again.

"The other one's going to surprise you," he said. "And don't say a word to anyone about him unless he turns out to be guilty. If you do, he'll sue your ass off."

"Dan, I know the rules."

"Yeah, I guess."

"So?"

He hesitated a few more seconds before saying, "Rick Wilde."

"The movie star?"

Stupid question, she told herself before all three words were even out. What other Rick Wilde would he mean?

But Rick Wilde was almost as big a name in Hollywood as Billy Brent.

"Why him?" she asked.

"Well, he and Billy used to be buddies until they were both up for the lead in *Chasers.*"

"Ah."

She hadn't known Rick Wilde had been after that role, but she could see why he'd be upset about not getting it.

From her research for her interview with Billy, she knew that *Chasers* had done incredible box office. It had been Billy's most successful film to date.

Still, a major film star hiring a hit man to kill a rival seemed awfully far-fetched.

On the other hand, they *were* talking Hollywood.

"Since *Chasers,*" Dan continued, " Rick Wilde's apparently gotten it into his head that every role he *really* wants ends up going to Billy.

"But I'll be surprised if he's actually the one behind the contract. I figure it's far more likely to be someone here in New York. So what we have to do now is start working our way through the list of potential suspects. Unless,'' he added, ''Lydia *does* manage to come up with the killer's name. Then we'd still have a chance at nailing him.''

''Do you think she will?''

Dan's shrug said probably not.

''So, assuming she doesn't, how do we figure out who's guilty?''

''Well, it's not an exact science. Basically, we just meet with them. Talk to them. Ask questions and listen to their answers. Watch their body language. And hope it's not long before one of them says something that reveals more than he—or she—intended to.''

She tried to look as if that all seemed perfectly reasonable to her, but she must not have quite pulled it off because Dan said, ''Trust me, it works. Sooner or later, we'll get lucky. And since your nickname used to be Miss Questions, well, I'm sure you'll be a help.''

She couldn't keep from smiling, partly because he'd obviously really been listening when she'd told him about her brothers, and partly because he'd admitted she wasn't a total liability.

That was definitely a major breakthrough.

Once she'd managed to lose the smile, she said, ''And how do we convince these people that they want to meet with us?''

''By explaining why it's in their best interest.''

''Which it really isn't, right?'' she asked. ''I mean,

it definitely isn't for whoever of them did hire the killer.''

''No. But whoever did won't want to seem uncooperative. And with each of them, it's just a matter of slanting our approach the right way.''

''Which is...?''

''Well,'' Dan said slowly, ''the most important rule is to stick as closely as possible to the truth. The less we lie, the less chance that one of the lies will come back to haunt us. So we'll tell them about the contract on Billy, but we'll put different spins on the story, focusing on something that'll make each one figure he, or she, will be better off talking to us than not.''

''For example?''

''I don't really have one for you. Since I was hoping to get my hands on the killer, and learn who'd hired him that way, I haven't given approaching the suspects much thought. But we'll basically be playing things by ear. So you'll just have to follow my lead.''

She nodded, wishing he'd say that she'd undoubtedly have some good ideas, that he wasn't assuming she'd only be following his lead.

When he didn't, she told herself not to expect too much all at once.

''And when we figure out which of them is behind the contract...?'' she asked, careful to say *when,* rather than *if*—despite what she was thinking.

''Then we get the hit called off,'' Dan said. ''And turn whoever paid for it over to the police. It'll be up to them to find the hit man, but at least he won't still be after Billy."

"Ah," she said, although she doubted they could ensure this all play out as easily as he was making it sound.

In fact, if she didn't know Dan was an expert, she wouldn't believe they had a prayer of doing it at all.

"Given that we'll be here for a bit," he said, "I'm going to rent a car. I hate relying on cabs. And I don't know whether you were listening while I was talking to Lydia…"

When he paused, she could tell that he figured she'd probably been hanging on every word.

There was that damn lack of trust again.

Of course, she wasn't entirely innocent in the eavesdropping arena, but even so…

"No, I wasn't listening," she told him, trying to sound as if it was something she'd never even dream of doing again.

He didn't look as if he entirely believed that, but he simply said, "Well, I told her I wanted a different place to stay, asked her to have someone call around and find a bed-and-breakfast."

"Why a B and B?"

"Because when someone might be watching you, smaller is better. Makes it easier to spot the someone."

His answer made her wish she hadn't asked the question.

As evenly as she could, she said, "You mean that

you figure, if the killer is keeping an eye on this hotel, he'll follow us to wherever we go next?''

''Hopefully not. The desk has my credit card imprint, so when we're ready to leave I can just call down and tell them to put the charges through. That way, there won't be any standing around waiting in the lobby. And if things go well, even if our boy *is* keeping an eye on the hotel, we'll be able to clear out without his knowing.''

She merely nodded, wishing she could contribute more to their planning. Or contribute *anything,* to be accurate.

Suddenly she didn't feel half as confident that she'd be having any good ideas. Maybe she *would* end up merely following Dan's lead.

That wasn't a happy thought, so she tried to make herself feel better by deciding that, considering he was an expert, he probably didn't want much of a contribution from her.

''I was figuring that you'd be going home,'' he continued. ''When I talked to Lydia, I mean. So I only asked her to book one room.''

She tried to ignore the sudden cottony sensation in her mouth, which became even harder to do when he added, ''Would you have a problem if we just left things like that?''

''You're saying continue the Mr. and Mrs. charade?''

''Uh-huh. I'd feel better if I could keep a close eye on you.''

'Right. I'd feel better too.''

That was at least partially true.

She'd feel safer, physically. Emotionally speaking, however, she wasn't sure how she'd feel.

Spending another couple of nights, or possibly weeks, in the same room as Dan, aware that he wasn't much more than an arm's reach away, might not exactly be conducive to a relaxing night's sleep.

"Good." He flashed a smile that made her certain a relaxing night's sleep wouldn't be in the cards.

"But you'd better fill me in on a few details," she told him, glad to discover that her brain was still at least semifunctioning. "Like where we live, for example. People in B and Bs tend to be a lot less impersonal than hotel staff."

"You're right. Okay, then, we live in Hartford, Connecticut."

"Do we really? I mean, do *you,* really?"

"Well, that's where RCI headquarters is, so I keep an apartment there. I don't use it all that much. Have you ever been to Hartford?"

"No."

"Then if somebody starts asking questions about it, just let me answer them. As for anything else, well, I'm sure we can deal with whatever comes up. Oh, and when Lydia gets back to me I'll ask her to check that whatever place they've booked has a data port."

"Thanks."

"And two beds, of course."

"Right. Of course," she said, feeling her face flushing and hoping it wasn't obvious.

Sharing a room with him was going to be bad enough. But the thought of sharing a bed with him and not...well, that would certainly constitute a major test of her willpower, and she had trouble imagining it would be up to the challenge.

"While we're waiting to hear from Lydia," Dan added, "why don't we see if we can get some lunch from room service. What would you like?"

"Oh...Caesar salad, maybe?"

"And a beer?"

"Sure."

As he was ordering a couple of Caesars plus a steak sandwich, Mickey packed up her camera and laptop so she'd be ready to go whenever he was.

Once she'd gotten organized, Dan began to fill her in on the New Yorkers Billy figured might want him dead.

"I made notes on what he said about everyone mentioned," he explained. "Then I did some research while I was at his retreat and came up with a shortlist of four."

She listened while he told her a bit about each of the people Billy thought were viable "suspects." By the time he gotten through them and was on to his shortlist, she was having trouble keeping the details straight.

Apparently, Billy had more enemies than friends, and it didn't sound as if determining who was behind the contract was going to be even remotely easy.

She was still trying to get all the players sorted

out in her head when room service arrived. Then, just as they finished eating, Dan's cellular rang.

"Dan O'Neill," he answered.

"Hi, Lydia," he said a couple of seconds later, shooting Mickey a meaningful glance.

She could feel her pulse beginning to race. Had Lydia learned the hit man's identity?

This time around, she was more than ready to eavesdrop, but it didn't get her far. Aside from asking Lydia to check about the data port and the two beds, Dan basically just listened to what she was telling him.

Finally he scribbled something onto the little pad the hotel had provided and said, "Don't worry about it. I know you did your best."

Mickey's hopes plunged.

"Yeah," he added. "If any of your other leads *do* produce something, call me right away. Regardless of the time."

As he set his cell phone down, Mickey said, "I gather she didn't come up with a name to match the picture."

"Actually she did," Dan told her. "But only a first name. Or it could be a nickname. Whichever, his street name is Turk, he lives someplace in Manhattan and has a reputation as one of the best hit men in the country."

"How did she find out even that much?"

He shrugged. "I didn't ask, but our research operatives can connect with any number of informants in the big cities. In most of the smaller ones, too. So that was probably her approach. At any rate, she's going to keep digging and might come up with more. But the other important thing she found out is that our boy's got no police record. Which means he's smart as well as good."

Mickey nodded, thinking that if he was one of the best she was probably lucky to still be alive.

She'd just have to hope her luck held.

EACH TIME A PHONE RANG at the hotel's desk, Turk went onto high alert. So far, however, he'd been disappointed.

The only time Room 803 had called down it was to order something to eat, and the fact nothing was happening had him firmly mired in a fresh pit of anger.

When a job dragged on, it really messed with his mind. And this was one of the worst. Aside from anything else, having been forced to spend most of last night on a plane had left his brain rough around the edges.

Or was that only his way of rationalizing how he could have been careless enough to let the O'Neill woman even see him at NBS, let alone take his damn picture?

He told himself not to start dwelling on that again. What was done was done.

Besides, the O'Neills would eventually lead him to Billy Brent, and then he could stop worrying about anything else. He'd be able to whack the three of them at once, which would tie everything up with no more effort required.

Eventually, after way too many false alarms, the desk clerk answered the phone and then nodded to him. He rose and started across the lobby, keeping his newspaper open in case he had to hide his face behind it at any second.

The theory that you could never be too careful had always served him well, and even though one of the O'Neills might be calling the desk, the other one could be anywhere.

Like on the way down here, for example.

He glanced at the elevator indicators. When he saw that that they were both still reading "one," he turned his attention to the stairwell door.

It was closed, but that could change in the blink of an eye.

Reaching the desk as the clerk hung up, he shot the fellow an expectant glance.

"They're checking out," he said.

"When?"

"I think in a couple of minutes."

He took a folded C-note from his pocket and slipped it across the counter.

The man tucked it away before saying, "There's something else."

"Oh?"

He felt like grabbing the clerk by the throat and telling him he'd already been paid more than enough. But this wasn't the time to make a scene, so he simply produced another hundred.

Holding on to it, he said, "What else?"

"He asked me where the closest car rental place was."

"And where is it?"

"Near the corner of West Forty-sixth and Sixth."

"And that's all?" he said, putting the bill on the desk but resting his fingers across it.

When the desk clerk nodded, he removed his hand.

"There won't be any trouble, will there?" the fellow said, quickly reaching for the money. "Here in the hotel, I mean?"

"No. There won't be any trouble. And if anyone ever asks, you never saw me. Right?"

"Right."

He inched his jacket open just far enough to give the guy a glimpse of his gun—which he thought of as his "insurance move"—then he turned and started toward the ladies' room.

Another of his tried-and-true theories was that if something worked once you should stick with it. And there hadn't been a lot of traffic through the lobby, so the risk of some babe wanting to use the can within the next few minutes wasn't high.

Besides, if one did it would be no big deal. He'd just look confused, apologize, and get the hell out.

With the door of the john cracked open, he could see what he needed to, and it wasn't long before the O'Neills emerged from the stairwell.

Daniel was toting a couple of cases. Wifey had her laptop and camera bag.

His gaze locked on the bag and a fresh surge of

anger seized him. He'd like to shoot her right here and now, then grab that bag and take off.

But there was just no way. He'd have to kill both of them, plus the desk clerk for good measure, and he'd bet his mother's life that O'Neill was carrying.

Hell, the missus probably was too.

Considering that she'd gone to Billy's retreat with a gun, he had to assume she didn't go anywhere without it.

Besides, a hotel lobby didn't make for a good setting for that sort of action. The whole effing area would be crawling with cops in a matter of minutes.

And hadn't he already thought through the problem of those pictures?

Hadn't he decided that they weren't really a problem, that they couldn't cause him any serious trouble?

Of course he had. But even so, he'd still very much like to get his hands on that camera bag.

Telling himself to be patient, he watched Daniel O'Neill look carefully around the lobby, empty except for the desk clerk. Then he and the missus started rapidly toward the rear exit.

Dammit, he'd known they might go that route, but he'd been hoping they wouldn't.

His car sitting out on the front street, and them heading the opposite way, didn't add up to good news.

He hesitated, but he knew better than to start second-guessing himself. Even though he hated the thought of letting them out of his sight, for any time at all, if they were renting a vehicle he'd undoubtedly be needing his.

Since he really had no choice, he gave them long enough to get outside, then raced to the back door and pushed it open far enough to see that they were walking in the direction he expected.

That done, he sprinted to the front entrance and dashed across the street, not even taking time to give the finger to the half-dozen morons who honked at him.

He ran to his car, climbed in and got going, figuring he should be able to intercept the O'Neills at the next cross street.

And sure enough, when he turned the corner there they were.

Breathing more easily, he simply kept them in sight until they got to the rental place. Then he pulled up to the curb.

Reaching into the floor of the back seat, he removed the blanket that concealed the sports bag he kept handy.

Oh, he knew that leaving anything in a car was just asking for it to be stolen. But having to get stuff out of the trunk could sometimes be a problem. Besides, most thieves would break into the trunk as well as the car.

He dug what he wanted out of the sports bag, and a couple of minutes later he was wearing a different shirt, glasses he didn't need, and the cool baseball hat he'd picked up a month or so ago that had a ponytail attached to the back.

In some situations, it was better to look like a long-haired freak than like himself.

Since he figured he still had time to spare, he dug out his fake mustache and the jar of makeup glue.

Even after he'd finished fiddling with that, the O'Neills still hadn't reappeared.

When they finally did, he watched them stow their gear into one of the cars on the tiny lot—a silver import.

Then, once they'd driven off, he let a few cars pass him before pulling out into the traffic again.

He was an absolute master at tailing someone without being seen. Knew all the tricks. Even had a nondescript gray car, specifically because it wasn't the sort that people noticed.

He drummed his fingers on the steering wheel as he drove, feeling better now.

And he'd be feeling better still once the O'Neills *did* lead him to Billy Brent.

CHAPTER ELEVEN

THE BED-AND-BREAKFAST Lydia had chosen proved to be in the heart of Chelsea—a three-story brownstone on West Twentieth.

While Dan was filling out the registration card, for "Mr. and Mrs. O'Neill," the owner rambled on about the place. The architectural style was Italianate, she told them, and it had been built in 1850.

"It was really run-down when my husband and I bought it," she continued, "and we spent over a year turning it into what you see now."

"A lot of work, huh?" Mickey said.

"A ton of it. And if we'd realized how hard putting ensuite bathrooms into old construction would be, I don't know whether we'd have even taken it on. I'm sure we sent at least one of the plumber's children through college."

"I can imagine," Mickey told her. "My parents renovated our house when I was a kid, and everything they did just seemed to lead to more work."

Dan glanced at her, wondering if she was actually interested in the woman's story or just managing to sound that way.

As for him, the only thing he was interested in

was whether or not their friend, Turk, had tailed them here.

He'd kept a close watch in the rearview mirror, and hadn't spotted the guy, but that didn't guarantee anything. And if Turk had been lurking around that hotel, he certainly wouldn't have just stood there and watched them leave.

If wanting those pictures wasn't motivation enough, he also had to figure they might touch base with Billy somewhere along the line. And Turk would want to be there if they did.

Refocusing on what he was doing, Dan signed the card and handed it to the owner.

''Hartford,'' she said, glancing at it. ''I've been there. We did a tour of Mark Twain's house. I *am* thinking of the right city, aren't I?''

''Definitely.''

''We used to travel so much I sometimes confuse what's where, but I remember being fascinated by that house. The old telephone booth in the front hall and everything.''

''Uh-huh,'' Mickey agreed. ''We take all of our out-of-town visitors to see it.''

Dan gave her an ''Oh, really?'' look, thinking that she'd have made a good actress.

The woman smiled, then turned her attention back to him, saying, ''Here are your keys. The silver ones are for the front door and the bronze one is for your room. Now, if you'll come with me I'll show you to it.''

As she turned and started down the hall, he gestured for Mickey to follow along first.

Then he bent to pick up their cases, aware of his Glock pressing reassuringly into his waist.

Mickey, he knew, had the gun they'd brought from Billy's retreat in her purse. And he'd stashed that Magnum Turk had left behind in the trunk of the rental. Just in case.

Years ago, during one of his worst ever days as a cop, he'd gotten careless and ended up with a couple of scumbags stuffing him into his car's trunk.

They'd driven him to a swamp a few miles outside of New Orleans, intending to kill him. And when they'd opened the trunk to pull him out, the fact that he kept a gun hidden in there had come as a major surprise to them.

Telling himself it was better to forget about negative experiences, he went back to thinking about the guns that Mickey and he had right here and now.

He hoped they wouldn't need them, but experience told him not to count on it.

Before heading after the two women, he had a final look out onto the street. He was far from feeling completely reassured that Turk wasn't out there. He hadn't forgotten that Lydia had said Turk was one of the best at what he did.

Of course, under normal circumstances that wouldn't be particularly disconcerting, because Dan was one of the best at what *he* did.

However, these were hardly normal circumstances. And he'd been deviating from his usual M.O., despite knowing it wasn't a wise idea. But he didn't generally have to worry about anyone except himself, and having Mickey along made a big difference.

If he'd been on his own, he'd have checked out every inch of that hotel lobby—as well as the entire block of the street—before he'd left. And if their hit man had been anywhere within shouting distance, he'd have found him.

As things had stood, though, he'd been far more concerned about getting Mickey away safely than about making sure their killer was nowhere in the vicinity. If old Turk had been hanging around, he might have been hoping for a chance to shoot her and grab her camera, which had made a rapid exit seem like the best plan.

When they started up the stairs, Mickey right in front of him, he couldn't force his gaze from her swaying hips.

Not even after he told himself that staring at them was a really dumb thing to do. Seeing how desirable she was, only made him want her more.

And, dammit, he didn't want to want her.

Only a fool would let himself want something he could never have. Not on any long-term basis.

As for the short-term…well, that might be a possibility. The way he'd caught her watching him a few times had told him so.

But his instincts had warned him that getting into something short-term with Mickey Westover would be a very bad idea. That in the end, it would only leave both of them wishing they'd steered clear of each other.

He forced his gaze from her as they continued up the staircase, and for some inexplicable reason his thoughts drifted to Chelsea Everett.

She was a tactical driving instructor at RCI—an unusual occupation for a woman, but one she'd come by honestly.

The story she always told was that her father, retired racing champion, Slick Everett, had taught her to drive practically before she could walk.

At any rate, even before Chelsea had gotten married a few months back, they'd never been anything more than buddies. But whenever he had some downtime in Hartford they'd always try to get together for a couple of beers.

Sometimes, he'd just stop by RCI on spec, to see if she was around. And when he did that he'd often find her tinkering with a car engine and quietly singing the same old song to herself.

It was one of her mother's favorites, she'd told him the time he'd asked about it, and he didn't know what it was called, but there was a line in it that said, "A taste of honey is worse than none at all."

As they reached the second floor he let his eyes return to Mickey, suddenly realizing why he'd started thinking about Chelsea or, more precisely, about that song of hers.

Mickey might be damned annoying at times, but he knew, deep down, that he was going to miss her after she walked back out of his life. And he didn't want to make that missing any worse than it would already be.

"Here we are," their hostess said, stopping to unlock one of the four doors opening onto the hall.

The room faced the back, which was both good and bad, but under these particular circumstances he figured it was more bad. With Turk's whereabouts unknown, he'd prefer being able to check the street at will.

However, since the owner had mentioned being fully booked, there was no point in saying anything.

Mickey looked in and told her the room was lovely.

"I'm glad you think so. There are extra towels in the bathroom cabinet, and if you need anything else just let me know."

"Thanks," Dan said.

After giving them a quick nod, the woman headed back toward the stairs.

Dan followed Mickey inside and closed the door.

The first thing that struck him was that there were no chairs, only two double beds, two bedside tables, and a TV set.

The second thing was that, although the room was large, the beds pretty well filled it. There was barely enough space to walk between them.

Obviously, they'd been placed the way they were so that if someone wanted to push them together to make one enormous bed it wouldn't be difficult.

That observation kicked his imagination into high gear. Suddenly he was visualizing himself in the darkness next to Mickey. Listening to her breathing and smelling her intoxicating scent.

Jasmine and four-o'clocks.

Man, oh, man, he'd spend the entire night lying awake thinking about the Garden District.

''It really is a nice room, isn't it?'' she said.

Then she gave him one of her incredible smiles, and he knew there was no way in the world that if he was lying next to her in the darkness he'd be thinking about the Garden District.

DAN CHANGED INTO a pair of decent pants and a clean shirt, while Mickey went into the bathroom and emerged a few minutes later wearing a dress, which he couldn't help noticing revealed an extremely shapely pair of legs.

She apparently noticed him noticing, because she said, ''I forgot to bring pantyhose. Do I look okay without them?''

''Fine,'' he said, making himself look away and start unpacking the rest of his things.

Since they were both traveling light, getting organized took virtually no time. And that was just as well, because the longer he spent in the room with her the smaller it seemed to be growing.

If it shrank much more, he wouldn't be able to move without touching her, which he had absolutely no intention of doing.

As he'd been reminding himself with increasing frequency, after this job was over they'd never see each other again. So it made a whole lot of sense to continue not letting things become too friendly.

That way, neither of them would have any major regrets when they parted ways.

On that thought, he dismissed the subject from his mind. Entirely and permanently.

He did his best to, at least.

When Mickey picked up her camera case and glanced at him expectantly, he said, ''You don't want to take that along.''

For a second, she eyed him as if she couldn't figure out why he'd say something so dumb.

Then she said, ''Sure I do. I take it everywhere. I never know when I might see a terrific shot.''

''Fine, but today it would probably get in the way.''

''In the way? Dan, it's a camera, not an elephant.''

He was about to explain that she'd likely find herself posing as something other than a photographer, and that was why it would get in the way.

For good measure, he'd point out that she wouldn't be happy if she ended up having to leave it in the car. Not when there were as many vehicles broken into every day in New York City as there were bricks in the Empire State Building.

But before he'd opened his mouth, he started thinking about how stubborn she was.

If she decided she didn't like his reasoning, they'd be into a big debate about whether the damned camera went with them or stayed here. And assuming their previous arguments were anything to go by, the discussion would take forever and she'd end up winning it. He might as well save the time and effort this one would require.

After congratulating himself on being a man who learned from experience, he said, "So you're ready to hit the road?"

She seemed surprised that he'd dropped the camera issue, but just said, "Uh-huh. Who are we starting with?"

"Well, with any of the people on my shortlist."

"You really don't have any sense of which one is the most likely?"

"Uh-uh. Not without having met them. I can't even be sure it's one of those four. They're my best bets, but you can never completely rule out the dark horses."

"And Billy didn't seem to have a...well, *favorite* isn't the right word, but you know what I'm saying."

"If he did, he wasn't telling. He just kept repeating that it could be any one of a whole lot of people."

"Maybe he thought that if he gave you his best guess, he'd influence your thinking."

"Maybe," he agreed, although he doubted that would have even occurred to Billy.

"Anyhow, as I said," he added, "we'll have to meet them before we'll have much of a feeling for what's what. So unless your intuition's saying something..."

He eyed her hopefully, ready to take any help he could get.

There wasn't any forthcoming, however. She merely shook her head and said, "I'm afraid not."

"Then it really doesn't matter who we try to catch up with first."

"Try to catch up with? You mean we don't phone ahead? Make appointments?"

"Mickey..." he said, almost certain she was teasing. Surely she'd realized that, in a situation like this, the element of surprise could only help.

"I was joking," she said, giving him a smile.

"I knew that," he told her.

The look she shot him suggested she didn't entirely believe him, but all she said was, "Speaking of phoning people, it just occurred to me that I should make a quick call before we leave. If that's okay with you, I mean. My phone tends to misbehave in a moving car."

"Sure. Go ahead. Another minute or two won't make any difference."

And it would give him a chance to check out the street while she was still up here in the room.

He was about to say that he'd wait for her outside when she flashed him another of her great smiles.

Somehow, this one managed to glue his mouth shut and his feet to the floor, and he ended up silently standing where he was while she reached for her cellular, saying, "My parents knew I was going to Vancouver Island and they'll be expecting to hear that I got home safely. Don't look at me like that," she added.

"Like what?"

"As if I was eight years old. They just worry about me. You know how parents are."

When he nodded, she began punching in a number and said, "They'll really be surprised to hear I'm in New York."

"I'll bet."

After finally getting his feet moving again, he discovered that they refused to take him toward the door. So, instead, he strode over to the window and gazed down into the tiny courtyard below—the phrase "You know how parents are" echoing in his ears.

Clearly her parents came from a different mold than his.

He wasn't sure that his had ever expected him to check in. As a child, let alone as an adult.

Oh, he liked to think that his mother had, when he was really young. Although, since he had no recollection of it, maybe not.

There'd never been any controlling his brother, so she might have just assumed her younger son would be the same and hadn't bothered to try.

Or maybe she'd been in no position to try.

She'd always worked long hours, so he and Sean had basically looked after themselves.

As for his old man…well, Patrick O'Neill had been happiest when neither of his sons was anywhere around. That was the only time they weren't getting on his nerves.

"Hi, Mom," Mickey said.

He couldn't stop himself from turning to look at her.

"Well, no, actually I'm not. I'm in New York."

Whatever her mother said in response made Mickey smile.

This one went straight to his heart.

He swore to himself, thinking that nothing about their situation was good. Not the way he was feeling about her—despite his best efforts to be feeling nothing at all—and definitely not this magically shrinking room with its too-close-together beds.

Hell, he wasn't a saint. Far from it.

But how many times did he have to tell himself that Mickey was the sort of woman who'd expect too much from a relationship? More than he was prepared to give. More than he *could* give. He just knew she was.

"Well, I didn't manage to connect with Billy Brent at his retreat," she was telling her mother, "because he turned out to be in New York. So now I'm here, too. Courtesy of the *Post.*"

That almost started him laughing.

He supposed she could honestly claim that she wasn't lying, but she was certainly putting an interesting spin on the truth.

Of course, unless she wanted to get her parents worried sick, she could hardly admit that she was really here because she was after an exclusive on a contract killer. Or that she'd already come face-to-face with him.

"I don't know for sure," she said. "It depends on

how things go. I haven't actually got a meeting with Billy set up yet, and— Oh, okay.'' After a brief pause, she said, ''Hi, Dad.''

Dan turned back toward the window, not wanting to see her smile yet again and reflecting that he hadn't spoken to his father since that row at his mother's funeral.

Every now and then he thought about calling.

A few times, he'd even picked up the phone.

Then he'd start thinking that they'd probably just end up sniping at each other, so what was the point?

''No, I'm really not sure how long I'll be here,'' Mickey was saying. ''I'll call again in a couple of days—I'll probably know by then. Or you can always phone me.''

He exhaled slowly, now thinking about how long it had been since he'd talked to his brother, the only member of his family he really did make an effort to keep in touch with.

But you couldn't just always phone a resident of San Quentin. No more than Sean could just always phone a brother who, at any given time, might be virtually anywhere in the world.

''I know, Dad,'' Mickey said. ''I love you, too.''

His chest suddenly felt tight, and no matter how hard he tried, he couldn't stop wondering how he'd feel if she said that to him.

MICKEY LOOKED across the car at Dan, glad that he was the one driving.

She found heavy traffic terribly frustrating, and

this trip up Fifth Avenue was more of a crawl than a drive. But they were closing in on their destination.

They'd reached Central Park and were inching their way north alongside it, which, of course, put them in the heart of the Upper East Side—*the* residential district of Manhattan. It practically smelled of wealth.

Had Upper East Side dollars paid for the contract on Billy, though? Or had that particular money come from elsewhere?

Now that their primary focus was on figuring out who was behind that contract, she was doing her best to make her mind work like a detective's, and hoping she proved to have an aptitude along that line.

"What are you thinking about?" Dan asked, glancing over at her after he'd stopped for a red light.

"Oh, I was just wondering if we're going to get lucky right off the bat."

"Don't set yourself up for a disappointment. This could take a while."

Hmmm. There was that imprecise little phrase again. Earlier, he'd said they could be here in New York for "a while." And for however long that ended up amounting to, she'd be with him practically twenty-four hours a day.

Telling herself she'd already spent more than enough time worrying about that, she turned her thoughts to his shortlist of New York suspects.

One of them was an embittered ex-agent named Hector Washington.

Hector had worked his butt off for Billy in the

early years, then Billy had promptly fired him when he'd decided he'd ''outgrown'' the man.

The two were currently engaged in a lawsuit, and Dan figured the agent might have decided he'd do better fighting the estate than Billy Brent in person.

The second name on the list was Maria Rosemount, a former girlfriend who'd had a child with Billy. The little girl was five now, and Billy had always paid Maria generous child support. But while she claimed to have no hard feelings, something had made Dan think she might be the one.

He hadn't gone into the details of why he did yet, which was fine with Mickey. There were only so many facts that she could absorb at one time.

The other two names on his shortlist were those of Billy's ex-wife, June Brent, and the couple's eighteen-year-old son, Cole.

Dan had said that while he wasn't about to tell Billy he suspected the kid, he definitely wanted to size him up; Mickey's gut reaction to that had been that Dan was really reaching.

Initially, the idea of an eighteen-year-old hiring a hit man at all, let alone one to kill his own father, had struck her as awfully far-fetched.

But as Dan had pointed out, it wouldn't be the first time a teenager had gotten involved in something like that. And the more he'd told her about Cole, the less improbable his suspicions had seemed.

Courtesy of Billy, his son apparently had access to virtually any amount of money he wanted, so he'd have had no problem coming up with enough to pay for the contract.

As far as his personality was concerned, he'd inherited his father's impetuous nature and poor-judgment genes. And on top of that, he harbored a whole lot of resentment toward Billy for—as he saw it—"deserting" him and his mother.

In reality, again according to Dan, Billy showed more responsibility toward them than he did in most areas of his life. He was never late with his alimony or child support checks, although that could be nothing more than a reflection of his bookkeeper's efficiency.

Still, he *did* make a point of seeing Cole at least some of the times he visited New York, and he had the boy stay with him in L.A. for a couple of weeks each summer.

To his son's way of thinking, however, none of that came anywhere near compensating for the divorce. So what they had in Cole Brent was an angry kid without a lot of self-control, who knew he stood to inherit if Billy died.

She shifted her train of thought to the inheritance aspect of the puzzle.

Was whoever wanted Billy dead basically after money? Was the primary motivation greed?

Since that was one of the logical possibilities, Dan and Billy had thoroughly discussed the issue of his beneficiaries—who they were and which of them knew he'd named them in his will.

Cole definitely did.

Billy had mentioned that, whenever the boy's behavior got particularly out of hand, he'd threaten to disinherit him.

Mickey didn't think that said much about the man's parenting skills, but the point was that Cole realized he'd gain financially if his father died.

All in all, once everything had been added together, she'd realized that Dan was right. It definitely was worth taking a good, hard look at Cole. In fact, based on what little she knew, she'd put him and his mother at the top of the list.

CHAPTER TWELVE

"ARE YOU STILL THINKING or are you daydreaming, now?" Dan asked, glancing across the car at Mickey once more.

Lord, did he really think daydreaming was possible when there were ten million details about their suspects running around in her head?

"Still thinking," she told him. "And thinking hard."

"Glad to hear it," he said.

Then he shot her a smile, which was all it took to start her pulse racing.

She certainly hoped that her time with him didn't end up amounting to too much. At least, that was what the sensible part of her hoped.

She forced her mind from Dan and back to the fact that, hopefully, they'd catch Cole and his mother in their apartment.

Academics weren't the boy's strength. In fact, his grades were absolutely atrocious. And apparently Billy had his limits. He wasn't prepared to donate a library or science lab to insure that one of the better colleges would accept his son despite the bad marks.

So Cole was spending July in school—getting special tutoring along with half a dozen other rich kids who had to do some extra work. And since the small private school the boy attended was within walking distance from where he and his mother lived, if he wasn't already home he soon should be.

Dan turned off Fifth Avenue and onto one of the Seventy-something streets, then pointed through the windshield, saying, "They live in that dark brick building up ahead."

While she eyed the elegant facade, with its burgundy canopied entrance and uniformed doorman, Dan pulled over to the curb. When she looked at him again, he was unclipping his cellular from his belt.

"I'm calling June Brent," he told her, punching in one of the numbers from his little electronic organizer.

"I realize I said that phoning ahead isn't the best way, but we can't just go barging into a place like this one. I'll have to convince her she wants to see us."

After a few moments of silence he said, "Mrs. Brent? We haven't met, but my name is Daniel O'Neill and I'm affiliated with a company called Risk Control International. I've just flown into New York because it's imperative that I speak to you in person."

Listening to him, Mickey wondered how she'd respond if a stranger called her out of the blue and gave her that line. It would definitely peek her curiosity.

"Mrs. Brent, please don't try to put me off.

There's something we have to discuss and it's critical that you see me immediately. In fact, I'm on my way to your place right now—with a colleague from the FBI."

Mickey almost choked.

She knew that "impersonating an officer of the law" was a very real charge, and she couldn't imagine that "impersonating a federal agent" was any less real.

"If it would make you feel better," Dan continued, "when we get there I'll give you the direct number of someone in the FBI. Someone you can call who'll verify that we're legitimate."

Dan! Mickey mouthed to him.

He covered the phone with his hand and whispered, "She won't ask for the number. No one ever does."

Before she could trot out the adage about there always being a first time, he was speaking to Mrs. Brent again, saying, "We're coming straight from the airport. And I can't stress enough that this is an urgent issue."

After a brief pause, he said, "Well, I don't want to frighten you, but Risk Control International is in the survival business. We keep people alive. And we have reason to believe your son's life is in danger."

This time, she shot him a look to ask how he could downright lie about something that would scare the daylights out of the woman.

He merely shrugged, then put his hand over the phone again and whispered, "Whatever works."

A second later he said to June Brent, "Yes, this *does* have something to do with your ex-husband. But my concern at the moment is for your son. Is he there with you now?"

He listened, then said, "Did he say *how* late he'd be staying at school?"

After another moment or two, he said, "No, I'm sure he's safe where he is. But does he have a cell phone?"

Mickey couldn't imagine he wouldn't. And sure enough, Dan said, "Good. Then why don't you call and tell him not to leave the building until he hears from you again. And stress that's it critical he stays inside. We'll be at your place in only a few minutes and I'll explain everything. In the meantime, it would be a good idea to ask your concierge to have a look at my ID when we arrive—just so you'll be absolutely sure about who we are."

He clicked off, then said, "The kid's staying late to play poker with his buddies."

"Fine, but let's discuss that *colleague from the FBI* bit. Are you trying to get me thrown in jail?"

"How do you think I should have explained you? Told her that you're an Arts and Entertainment journalist from *The San Francisco Post?*"

"But I—"

"Which reminds me," he interrupted, "you can't take your camera with you, so you'll have to put it in the trunk. That's the safest place."

"But—"

"Look, it just doesn't fit an FBI cover. The trunk's not ideal but it's better than the car."

"Dan, I—"

"There's no choice, Mickey. I'll tell the doorman we won't be long. With any luck, he'll just leave it parked out front."

She nodded reluctantly, thinking she should probably be grateful that he hadn't said *I told you so.* Because he *had* told her to leave it at the B and B.

Once he'd popped the trunk, she climbed out and put the camera bag into it. Then she slammed the lid closed, telling herself the odds of somebody prying it open while they were gone had to be really low.

When she got back into the car, Dan was on the phone again, listening to what whoever he was talking to was saying, so she occupied herself by reviewing his rationale for putting June Brent on his short-list.

Not that it really needed reviewing. Billy's ex had enough potential motives to fill a three-bedroom house.

When she'd married him, she'd given up her own fledgling acting career because he'd insisted that two actors in a family was one too many. After that, she'd spent years putting up with being the wife of a marginally crazy egomaniac.

Among other things, she'd suffered the humiliation of her husband openly cheating on her—and not only with Maria Rosemount—until, eventually, he'd decided to make the move to Hollywood and told her that she and Cole weren't going with him.

Not surprisingly, there was no mention of her in his will, but the terms of their divorce settlement gave her a lump-sum payment if he died, in lieu of future alimony.

Plus, according to the legal eagle Dan had consulted after talking to Billy, June could make a case for being entitled to a portion of the estate that had been accumulated before their marriage had broken up.

Mickey was curious about what the "portion" might amount to, but Dan didn't have even a ballpark number.

He'd said that, to come up with one, somebody would have to wade through the California and New York State case precedents, and he hadn't figured it was worth either the effort or the money. Not after Billy had told him that, while he and June were married, she'd taken out a whopping big life insurance policy on him.

Since she'd never let it lapse, that would provide her with a goodly sum on his death.

"So the bottom line is you *could* play baby-sitter for a couple of days?" Dan said into the phone, interrupting Mickey's thoughts. "I know it would be boring, but it wouldn't be for long."

After a moment's pause, he laughed, then said, "Okay, so if it turns out I do need you I'll call back within the hour. And thanks. I was hoping you'd be free."

"What was that about?" she asked as he clicked off.

''Just talking to a fellow named Wayne Richards. He's an RCI operative here in New York, and we might want his help.''

''For?''

''Cole Brent's life is in danger. His mother may decide he needs a bodyguard.''

''But his life isn't actually in danger.''

''Mickey, you're supposed to follow my lead, not argue with me. Remember that when we get to June Brent's apartment. And here,'' he added, digging into his pocket. ''Stick this in your purse.''

She flipped open the small, black leather case he handed her, and discovered a very genuine-looking FBI agent's badge inside.

''Is this real?''

''Does it look real?''

''Yes, but—''

''Mickey,'' he said, shaking his head. ''Has anyone ever told you that you worry too much?''

AS SOON AS the O'Neills turned onto East Seventy-sixth, Turk had been sure he knew where they were heading. After he'd taken the money to whack Billy Brent, the ex-wife's residence was one of the places he'd scoped out for future reference.

But when the silver rental stopped half a block short of the apartment building, it had given him pause.

What was going on?

Since there was an obvious way of learning that, he'd tucked his car in behind a double-parked delivery truck, then climbed out to check on what the O'Neills were up to—glad he was in disguise, even though they probably didn't suspect they were being followed.

They'd remained in their car, and with its tinted windows he couldn't see a damned thing inside.

Eventually, however, the missus got out and stashed her camera bag in the trunk.

That had certainly kicked his heart into overdrive.

He'd feel a whole lot better if he could get his hands on that camera. Especially if it turned out to be just a regular old-fashioned one. And if it had a role of partially used film inside. And maybe some exposed rolls in the bag.

Uh-huh. Knowing she hadn't done anything with those shots of him would definitely ease his mind. Because no matter how many times he told himself they didn't pose a serious danger, there wasn't any denying that they were significant loose ends. And loose ends made him nervous.

After she got back into the car, O'Neill started off again. They didn't go far, though. Just as he'd initially figured, they were paying the ex Mrs. Brent a visit.

As O'Neill stopped in front of her building's entrance, Turk drove on by and then pulled into a No Stopping zone to see what happened next.

Was this where they were hooking up with Billy?

It didn't seem likely, but you never knew. Could be that Billy and his ex got along better than the tabloids claimed.

The O'Neills had barely opened their car doors before a valet appeared and held his hand out for the keys. When Daniel relinquished them, Turk experienced one of those died-and-gone-to-heaven feelings. People who thought things were safe in car trunks were idiots.

The valet disappeared into the driver's seat, the O'Neills headed for the entrance to the apartment building and Turk slipped his car back into Drive.

There was no reason to follow the valet. He'd checked this place out thoroughly enough that he knew where the visitors' parking area was.

He also knew how to get into it without being observed, so all he had to do now was find a legal place to leave his own car. He'd never yet come back to where he'd left it and found it missing, but that happened if you got careless.

Aside from the car thieves who patrolled the streets you had to worry about being towed. The people who put up those Don't Even Think About Parking Here signs were a serious bunch.

After driving around for longer than he'd hoped he'd have to, he found a space a couple of blocks away. Once parked, he took his gun and a trusty screwdriver from the glove compartment and dug a couple of disposable latex gloves out of the sports bag in the back. Then, hoping to hell that the O'Neills hadn't just stopped by June Brent's place for a couple of minutes, he rapidly made his way to the visitors' parking.

Luck was on his side. The rental was still there.

He glanced casually around, establishing that no one was watching, then jammed the end of the screwdriver into the lock of the trunk and began to work it back and forth.

It took him less than sixty seconds to get it open.

He grabbed the camera bag, then paused, staring at the copy of *The New York Times* that was tucked up tight against the back wall.

Funny. It was as fat as a Sunday edition but this wasn't Sunday.

As soon as he began pulling it forward he realized there was more to his find than a newspaper.

Unfolding it, he discovered a gun lying in the center. And not just any gun.

It was his favorite piece. The Magnum he'd figured he'd lost forever. But O'Neill had brought it along and stashed it here. Probably in case he needed extra firepower.

He grinned to himself. The day had gotten off to one hell of a bad start, but it was shaping up very nicely.

AFTER DAN AND MICKEY introduced themselves, June Brent scrutinized the business card Dan gave her.

While she did, he sized her up.

He knew that, like Billy, she was somewhere around forty. However, she looked more like thirty—an extremely attractive thirty.

She put him in mind of a young Goldie Hawn and, baring the possibility that she was hiding an evil side, she wasn't the sort of woman most men would run around on and then dump. Of course, Billy wasn't most men.

Putting his card into her pocket, she glanced at Mickey once more but didn't ask to see her ID.

She simply said, "Why don't we go into the living room," then started across the foyer.

While he and Mickey followed along, he was thinking that not asking for any more ID said a lot about how much Billy's ex trusted her concierge.

Of course, it wasn't hard to understand why she would.

The man had not only closely inspected his RCI identity card, his driver's license and Mickey's FBI badge, he'd also asked her for photo ID to go with it.

Fortunately, she hadn't blinked an eye. She'd simply told him she was working undercover, and that the rest of the ID she had in her purse was phony.

Dan had felt like hugging her.

But he'd rather not still be feeling like hugging her now, five minutes later. It was an urge he wished to hell he didn't have.

It was also a most distracting one, and this was no time for distractions. He had to concentrate fully on the story he was about to give June Brent.

The white marble floor of her foyer led into an enormous living room, and when they reached it, she gestured toward one of the twin couches flanking the fireplace, inviting them to have a seat. Then she sat down on the other couch and eyed them expectantly.

Since she obviously wanted to cut directly to the chase, he said, "I should start by explaining how this situation we have arose. Someone put a contract on your ex-husband's life."

Her face showed absolutely no emotion.

"A contract on Billy," she said after a couple of beats. "If I told you that surprises me I'd be lying. I'm more surprised that nobody's killed him before now. But the part of this situation that concerns me is my son's safety, so let's get to why you said his life is in danger."

"I will in just a minute. There's a bit more background to fill in first."

She nodded, but her impatience was showing. It made him decide that while she might look like Goldie Hawn, she lacked that adorable quality.

"Billy learned about the contract and called my company for help," he continued. "For various reasons, I involved Special Agent Westover."

He glanced at Mickey, who nodded to June Brent while managing to look very official.

"At this point," he went on, "we have Billy in seclusion and we're tracking down the hit man. That brings us to where your son comes into the picture."

"Good."

"This killer is aware that Billy found out he was a target and sought protection. And our sources tell us that he's decided the best way to flush Billy out of hiding is to kidnap your son and play let's make a deal."

At that, June Brent's face lost most of its color. Then a look of suspicion crept over it.

"Your sources?" she said. "You're saying that this…killer tells people what he's doing?"

He'd been hoping she wouldn't question anything he told her, but they weren't going to be that lucky. She'd apparently toughened up from the days when Billy used to walk all over her.

"Even professional killers talk to a friend or two," he said. "Or divulge things in other ways. And that's all we need."

When she was silent, he added, "Look, grabbing your son is what the hit man has in mind. I can't go into details, but Special Agent Westover and I have the resources of the FBI and Risk Control International to draw on. We can learn just about anything we want to know."

"Then why haven't you learned who this hit man is?"

"We have," he told her. "His name is Turk. And as I said, we're in the process of tracking him down. But while we're doing that, we want your son to be safe."

He watched her closely as he spoke, but if she'd already known Turk's name there was nothing to indicate it.

Without another word, she rose from the couch and walked over to the windows, wrapping her arms around herself as if for comfort.

Seeing how obviously upset she was made him

feel a little guilty, which he definitely would not have been feeling if it weren't for Mickey.

That look she'd given him in the car, when he'd been talking to June Brent on the phone, had plainly said that she disapproved of his scaring the woman by saying her son was in danger when he really wasn't.

But hell, as he'd told her way back, RCI had only one rule and it was Don't Let The Client Get Killed.

Whether he liked Billy Brent or not, his job was to keep the man alive. If doing that meant temporarily frightening his ex-wife and son, then that's what he'd do.

Besides, for all he knew, neither June Brent's fear nor her distress was real. She'd been an actress before she'd married Billy, which meant it wouldn't be smart to take any of her reactions at face value.

Plus, he wasn't forgetting that both she and the boy were on his list of suspects.

If she had hired Turk, she'd know damn well that he wasn't going to try kidnapping Cole. The man was a professional. He wouldn't take her money, then intentionally cause her grief.

So was she truly upset or was this all an act?

He glanced at Mickey again.

She gave him a little shrug, letting him know they were having the same problem reading the woman.

Dan focused on June Brent once more, and as she continued to stare down at the street he began wishing he could walk over and join her in front of the window.

But what did he think he'd see? Turk standing in plain view on the sidewalk, looking up toward the apartment?

That was hardly realistic thinking.

If Turk *was* still following them, he'd do everything he could to keep them from being aware of him.

Finally June Brent turned and—her voice no longer even—said, "I should call the police. Shouldn't I?"

Dan had been expecting that, but the last thing he wanted was her phoning the cops when he'd just finished feeding her a load of manure and Mickey was sitting there posing as a federal agent.

"Let's discuss that in a minute," he said. "But first, did you do what I suggested and call Cole at school? Tell him not to leave?"

"Yes."

"Then may I make another suggestion?"

"Of course."

"Why don't I get in touch with an associate who lives here in New York."

"He's another security specialist?"

"Right. His name is Wayne Richards, and he's excellent at what he does.

"I'll arrange for him to go to the school and bring your son home. Then you can phone Cole and tell him to expect someone in half an hour or so."

"He could be there that soon?"

"I'll tell him sooner, if possible."

CHAPTER THIRTEEN

WHILE DAN SPOKE on the phone with Wayne Richards, Mickey surreptitiously watched June Brent, who was hanging on every word.

She looked so anxious that it seemed highly improbable she was the one behind the contract. And that was exactly what logic said, as well.

If she'd hired Turk, she wouldn't be worried about him harming her son. And since she was so obviously worried, she couldn't possibly have known Dan was mixing lies with his truths. Except that, since the woman had trained as an actress, *couldn't possibly* might be a touch strong.

After downgrading "highly improbable" to merely "improbable," Mickey turned her attention to Dan, then immediately told herself she should start wearing blinders.

Despite everything that was going on—and it was a very substantial everything—just looking at the man was enough to make her forget half the thoughts in her head.

That was totally unlike her, and it was undoubtedly because Dan was so unlike any other man she'd ever met, so different he was causing her brain to malfunction. It simply wasn't sure how to react to him, which was why her hormones had managed to gain control.

Yes, that definitely explained the problem. Now all she had to do was figure out how to solve it.

He was in the process of finishing up his call, and as soon as he clicked off, June Brent said, "Well?"

"It's set," he told her. "Just tell your son to wait inside the front door for Wayne."

Without another word, she picked up a cordless from the end table and pressed a speed-dial number.

"Cole, it's me again," she said after a few seconds.

"I'm sending someone to get you. His name is Wayne Richards and he'll be there in about half an hour."

There was a brief pause before she said, "I'll tell you all about it when you get here. And remember not to go outside. Not for any reason. He'll be coming in, so just wait near the door."

She frowned as she listened again, then said, "Cole, I *know* you're not a baby, but just do something the way I ask for once, okay? It'll make sense when I explain."

A moment later, she stiffly said, "I don't like that language, so please clean it up. I'll see you soon.

"Teenagers," she muttered, putting down the phone.

Her annoyed expression only lasted a few seconds, though. Then it was replaced by another worried one and she said to Dan, "You're sure he'll be all right until your associate gets there? This Turk person won't go into the school?''

''No. And we don't even know that he has it under surveillance. I'd just rather not take chances.''

''But in case he is there...as I said before, shouldn't I call the police? So they'll send a cruiser? I mean, a lot can happen in half an hour.''

Dan shook his head. ''First off, they wouldn't send a cruiser. Anything you told them would be pure speculation, which they don't waste their time on. And by involving them...''

''What?''

''It might not be the best idea,'' he said slowly.

''Why not?''

''Well, I won't say they'd make the situation worse...''

Mickey couldn't help thinking he was awfully good at this sort of thing.

He let the sentence hang just long enough to imply that making the situation worse was exactly what he figured they'd do, before he said, ''Look, if you contact them several things will happen. First off, the story would get leaked.''

''You mean by them? The police?''

''Uh-huh. We're talking a hired killer after Billy Brent. And the fact that the killer has made Billy's son a kidnapping target. There's just no way some cop wouldn't pass that along in exchange for whatever. And as soon as the media got wind of it, our hit man would go to ground, which would be fine if he'd drop out of the picture permanently. But sooner or later he'd resurface, and none of us would know where or when that was going to happen. So the danger to Cole…well, long story short, this whole mess would only be prolonged."

"Bloody media," June Brent muttered. "I hate them. They're nothing but a bunch of vultures."

Mickey kept her mouth tightly shut. She'd been called worse than a vulture.

"If you'd like my opinion…" Dan said.

"Yes. What is it?"

"I think the best thing you can do is hire a bodyguard. Have him stick with Cole twenty-four-seven. Do you have a spare room?"

She nodded.

"Well, I'm sure it wouldn't be for long. We'll have Turk in custody very shortly. And since Wayne Richards is between assignments at the moment…"

"What do you think?" the woman asked, turning to Mickey.

"I think it's good advice," she said.

When Dan gave her just the trace of a nod, her face began growing warm.

It made her desperately wish she didn't feel pleased by his approval. That she didn't feel so inordinately pleased, at least.

BEFORE WAYNE RICHARDS ARRIVED at the apartment with Cole, June Brent had decided it would be better if Dan told her son what was going on.

"He thinks I tend to exaggerate things," she'd explained. "And that I overreact. So if he figures a bodyguard is *my* idea, he'll put up a big fuss."

Dan was only too happy to oblige. The more he interacted with Cole, the better chance there'd be of figuring out whether the boy wanted his father dead.

As soon as June heard him at the door, she rushed into the foyer and gave him a big hug, which he obviously didn't appreciate. Dan and Mickey had followed along after her, but Dan hung back a little to get an impression of the kid.

He resembled Billy somewhat, tall and lanky with the same curly brown hair. His features weren't as chiseled, though, and he didn't have his father's confident—or probably *arrogant* was a better word—manner.

Of course, he was only eighteen.

When his mother introduced him, he was clearly more impressed at meeting Special Agent Mickey Westover than a second man from RCI, a company he'd never before heard of.

Dan got a little nervous when Cole began asking Mickey questions about the Bureau, but she proved to be a pretty good bull slinger. With three older brothers, there'd likely been a lot of cop shows on the Westovers' TV while she was a kid. But whatever the reason, she certainly sounded as if she knew what she was talking about.

They all finally ended up in the living room, and as Cole slouched into one of the wing chairs facing the fireplace, his mother said, "Mr. O'Neill's going to fill you in on what's happening."

The boy listened in silence, his expression saying he wasn't quite sure whether to believe the story.

"So this Turk?" he said after Dan had finished. "Like, he really thinks he can get to my dad by grabbing me?"

Dan nodded. "That's what I hear."

"Then you must be listening to some pretty dumb people, because if my father had to choose between me getting killed or him, I'd be dead in two seconds."

"Cole!" June said sharply.

He shot her a frosty glance. "You know that's true. It is," he insisted, looking at Dan again. "So if this dude's got half a brain, he wouldn't waste his time with me. I think your informants must have been smoking something."

Since there was nothing to gain by arguing, Dan merely said, "Well, as I told your mother, I don't like taking chances when we're talking about somebody's life. So I've suggested that, until we apprehend this guy, we give you a little protection."

"Like a gun?" he said, suddenly showing a whole lot of interest.

"No, I was thinking more like a bodyguard. Maybe, if Wayne's got some available time..."

He glanced questioningly in Wayne's direction, as if they hadn't discussed the matter earlier.

"Sure, I can hang with Cole for a day or two," Wayne said. "You'll probably have your man behind bars by then, right?"

"Wait a sec," Cole snapped. "Don't I get a say

in this? I don't want any baby-sitter. I can take care of myself.''

Dan glared at the kid for long enough to make him break eye contact, then quietly said, ''Grow up, Cole. The President of the United States has bodyguards. Do you figure you're a better man than him?''

WAITING FOR THE ELEVATOR in the hall outside June Brent's apartment, Mickey was dying to ask Dan whether he had either the mother or the son pegged as their guilty party. She didn't think it was one of them, but she wasn't the expert.

She managed to keep quiet until the brass door slid shut behind them, then said, ''Well?''

''It's not the kid,'' he told her. ''He might be a spoiled brat, but he didn't know a thing about the contract until I told him. As for the mother...''

He shrugged, then added, ''I didn't get any real sense that it *is* her, but I'm not entirely ruling her out yet. What did you think?''

''About the same as you,'' she said, wishing she'd picked up on something he hadn't. That wasn't a very likely thing to have happened, though.

''So who do we try next?'' she asked as they reached the ground floor. ''The ex-agent or the ex-girlfriend?''

Glancing at his watch, he said, ''It's almost dinnertime. Maybe we should grab something to eat and see how we feel after that. We might be smarter to get an early night and leave both of them for tomorrow.''

She nodded, a vision of that single room at the B and B front and center in her mind.

The prospect of spending another night in the same room as Dan was not something she wanted to think about. But since they'd decided it made sense to stick close together, in case…

Well, that wasn't something she wanted to think about, either, so as they walked out into the still-bright sunshine she did her best to stop thinking at all.

Dan had only called to have their car brought around a few minutes ago, but it was already waiting at the curb for them. The valet, standing beside it, looked as if he'd rather be somewhere else.

Once he spotted them, he seemed even more uncomfortable.

"Is there a problem?" Dan asked as they neared him.

"Yes, sir, I'm afraid so. Someone broke into your trunk."

Her Nikon! Mickey felt downright ill.

She watched Dan stride toward the rear of the car, only too aware that he'd been right and she'd been wrong.

Turk *had* tailed her from NBS, because he wanted to get his hands on her camera. And he'd continued following them from the hotel to the bed-and-breakfast, then on to here, just waiting for his chance.

Dan opened the trunk and reached inside, picking up a copy of the *Times,* then tossing it back down and slamming the lid shut.

It bounced open again.

"The thief forced it," the valet said. "The lock's a goner. I haven't called the police," he continued, "but I can if you like. They don't give any priority to things like this, though."

"No, don't bother," Dan told him.

"Let's go," he added to Mickey.

As she climbed in, he started the engine, saying, "We can't drive around with that lid banging up and down. We'll have to go back and get another car."

She nodded, but her mind was still primarily on her stolen camera. Even though it was insured, claims took time. And she needed a replacement immediately.

It was just lucky she'd forgotten about calling the place where she'd rented her car on Vancouver Island. If she'd told them to switch their charges from her Visa to her MasterCard, she'd have maxed it out too.

Telling herself that forgetfulness wasn't always a bad thing, she looked over at Dan, saying, "There's no chance it wasn't Turk, is there?"

"Oh, there's a small one. A lot of cars get broken into in New York. But the odds that it *was* him..."

"Are roughly ninety-nine percent?"

"That's probably a good estimate."

Of course, she'd already known it had almost undoubtedly been Turk. And since she really wasn't eager to ask yet another question—especially not the one that kept poking at the edge of her mind like a dull knife—she simply turned around in her seat and sat staring through the rear window as they headed down the street.

She didn't know what kind of car to even look for, though. And maybe he'd quit following them. After all, he'd gotten what he wanted. Unless her camera wasn't all he wanted.

The question she really didn't want to ask gave her another poke, a sharp one this time, and she couldn't help thinking that trying to ignore it was just burying her head in the sand.

After hesitating for another minute, she said, "Dan?"

"Uh-huh?"

"Do you remember what you said right after I showed you that picture of Turk?"

"I said a lot of things."

"Well, one of them was…you said he'd have followed me because he'd want to kill me before I could do anything with it. And you were obviously right. At least as far as the following part went."

"Being right doesn't always make me happy."

"No. But what I'm getting at…I'm thinking about the killing me part."

She'd been doing a pretty good job of ignoring the fact that she could end up dead, but it was getting harder and harder to do.

Dan pulled over to the curb and stopped, then looked at her—the depth of concern in his eyes telling her that she was right to be every bit as worried as she was.

"Look," he said, "I'm going to tell you the truth.

I don't think he'll be satisfied with just having your camera. It's damn likely he's still following us. And since he's careful enough that we haven't spotted him before now, he's not likely to suddenly get sloppy."

"But—"

"Just listen to me for a minute, Mickey, because I want you to be completely clear about where things stand.

"The man's a professional killer without a police record. That means he's smart, thorough and cautious. The sort of guy who, when he knows something could cause him problems, tries to take care of it before that can happen. And you could cause him problems. So things have reached the point...well, here's where we're at. I know I agreed to your staying, but you've got to go home now. No arguments about it this time. Not when we've seen for ourselves how good he is."

She looked through the windshield at nothing.

"You know I'm right, don't you?" Dan asked quietly.

"Maybe you are. But if I went home... Dan, I keep a business card inside my camera bag, with a note on the back saying there'll be a reward for its return."

"Oh, jeez. Exactly what's on the card?"

"The standard. My name, my title of photojournalist, the *Post*'s address and phone number."

He shook his head. "If he knows your name and where you work, he can get your home address in two seconds flat. In fact, he's probably done it already."

"Ah," she murmured, then nervously gnawed on her lower lip as the silence grew.

"So now," Dan finally continued, "we don't know whether you'll be in more danger if you go home or stay here."

"Then what do I do?" she asked, trying to ignore the fear that had gotten so strong it had begun eating away at her insides.

She waited again, listening to her heart thudding in her ears while Dan considered her question. This one, she didn't already know the answer to.

After several moments, he said, "If Turk is still keeping us under surveillance and you get on a plane for San Francisco, he might decide to put finding Billy on hold for the moment and head after you, which isn't something we can risk."

"So I stay here," she concluded, hoping she sounded a lot calmer than she felt.

Dan nodded. "You stay here. And we have to nail him. More than ever."

FROM THE FIRST MOMENT she'd realized that she was staring a front-page story in the face, the last place Mickey had wanted to go was home.

However, now that she knew she couldn't—not safely, at least—a sense of numbness had settled in on her.

While Dan exchanged the damaged rental car for another, and then while they found a restaurant and got something to eat, she'd been working at calming herself down.

But she hadn't succeeded. Her anxiety level was still sky-high. And the fact that Dan had lapsed into silence over dinner was certainly no help. It had left her to her own thoughts, every single one of which was about Turk and his gun.

In her imagination, it was the size of a small cannon. And she merely had to close her eyes to picture him standing around the corner of a building or hiding behind a parked car—ready to shoot her.

"Are you done?" Dan asked.

"Uh-huh," she said, glancing at her half-eaten burger and wondering if it was really as tasteless as it had seemed.

"Then let's head back to the B and B," he suggested. "Leave our other suspects till the morning."

She considered saying she'd like to stop at a camera store on the way, then decided that could wait until the morning, too.

Getting back to the relative safety of the bed-and-breakfast seemed like a far better idea than wandering around anywhere. And as uneasy as she might have been feeling about being alone in a room with Dan again, at this point she felt a whole lot more uneasy about being a potential target.

She slid out of the booth and followed him down the street to the car, trying not to see Turk's face on every man they passed. As they pulled away from the curb, and headed for Chelsea, she refused to let herself turn and look through the back window.

Yet she was certain their killer was somewhere behind them. Invisible but deadly.

When they reached their destination, Dan stopped out front and carefully looked up and down the street before saying, "I'll see you in, then find a place to park."

She swallowed nervously as he took his gun out of the glove box and stuck it into his belt, where it would be concealed by his jacket but handy in case he needed it.

He climbed out of the car, rapidly walked around to the passenger's side and then hurried her up the front steps and into the building.

"Well, hello," the owner said, poking her head around a corner when she heard the door close. "Have a nice afternoon?"

"Super," Mickey lied.

When Dan started to follow her down the hall, she said, "I'm fine. You don't have to come upstairs."

"Yeah, well..."

The fact that he followed her up to the second floor made her wonder if he was worried that Turk had climbed the drainpipe and snuck into their room.

He hadn't, of course, and once Dan had seen that he stepped back into the hall, saying, "I shouldn't be gone long."

"That's okay. I could use some time to work on my story."

Mickey watched him until he started back down the stairs, recalling his determined expression when he'd said they had "to nail" Turk and hoping he had a few concrete ideas about just how they were going to manage that.

Afraid he might not, she forced her brain into gear and began thinking as hard as she could.

CHAPTER FOURTEEN

THERE WASN'T A GOOD VIEW of the bed-and-breakfast's front door from where Turk had parked, so he was standing a couple of brownstones away, completely hidden by a staircase. Even though he was still wearing his disguise, he figured that was a good move.

He'd had to grab that camera when he'd been handed the opportunity. But neither O'Neill nor the woman would have the slightest doubt as to who'd taken it.

And that meant, regardless of whether they'd already been thinking he was following them or not, at this point they'd be certain of it.

He wasn't happy about that, but as long as he didn't let them spot him there'd be no problem with keeping on watching them. The B and B had no rear exit, so they couldn't leave without his knowing. And since he could get by for a couple of days with just catnaps in his car, he'd hang tight for the time being.

He hadn't given up on the hope that they'd eventually lead him to Billy. If they didn't…

Well, either way, he'd take care of them when the time and place were right.

As the door of the B and B opened, he stepped even farther behind the stairs and waited a few seconds before checking to see who'd come out. It was Daniel O'Neill, and he was striding over to his car.

The idea of tailing along to see where he was going was tempting. But not tempting enough to act on.

He was probably just heading off to find a legal parking space. Or, now that he knew he was under surveillance, he might be trying the decoy trick—hoping Turk would tail him so the woman could slip out with their luggage.

If that was the game, he wasn't playing. He simply watched the car pull away, thinking, not for the first time, how much he loved modern technology.

When they'd gone into that restaurant, he'd finally had a stretch of time to power up his laptop and do some research.

He hadn't managed to find much on O'Neill or the company he worked for, but he'd turned up enough to confirm that he wasn't up against an amateur.

Far from it. If he made any mistakes, he'd risk being in big trouble with O'Neill.

As for Michelle Westover, getting the goods on her had barely been a challenge. One look at that business card in her camera bag had told him he'd pegged her wrong, that she wasn't O'Neill's missus but a frigging reporter for *The San Francisco Post.*

That had sure given him a shock. It had also given him a starting place, though. By calling the paper and doing a little fast talking, he'd learned that she'd gone to Vancouver Island to interview Billy Brent, which had to mean that she and O'Neill barely knew each other.

How she'd ended up coming to New York with him was a mystery, but not one worth trying to puzzle his way through. As far as she was concerned, the only things he was interested in were those bloody shots she'd taken. And now he had them.

He'd had less trouble than he'd expected figuring out how to display what was on the camera's disk. Or chip. Or whatever.

It had merely been a matter of flicking a button to Play, then using an arrow to work his way through the pictures. The ones of him were still in the camera, which was the good news. The bad news was that he had no way of telling whether she'd made prints of them or sent them to her bloody paper.

He sure as hell wished he knew, because if his photograph ended up splashed all over the place his career would be finished, not to mention that he'd be running from the cops.

However, worrying wouldn't get him anywhere. He just had to hope he'd lucked out and she'd done nothing with the damned things. Nothing more than show them to O'Neill, at least.

That he'd had a look at them was a given, which meant the two of them knew what he looked like. And that left him absolutely no choice about taking them out. But it didn't matter, when he'd been intending to anyway.

He eyed the bed-and-breakfast again, toying with the thought of going in and whacking Michelle Westover right now. After all, he didn't need both of them to lead him to Billy.

It probably wasn't a smart idea, though.

First, he'd have to get inside without calling attention to himself. And even if he could manage that, he had no idea how many other people were in there.

No. Definitely not a smart idea.

He'd just have to be patient and keep an eye on the two of them for a little longer.

DAN FINALLY FOUND a place to park a couple of blocks away from the bed-and-breakfast, then started rapidly back.

Dusk was just beginning to settle in over the city, so there was still no difficulty seeing, and after he turned onto West Twentieth he kept a sharp eye out for Turk. But if the guy was around, undoubtedly the case, he was doing a good job of making himself invisible.

Nearing the front steps of the brownstone, he had a final look along the street.

He still didn't see anyone who even remotely resembled Turk, but he could practically feel the guy's eyes on him and it was making him more than a little uneasy. If he had to play cat and mouse he wanted to be the cat. And if he were on his own, he'd be tearing the damned street apart looking for Turk.

But he knew how frightened Mickey was, and the longer he took getting back the more worried she'd be. So as badly as he'd like to go on the offensive, he wouldn't. Not for the moment, at least.

He started up the front steps, thinking that she was cramping his style all to hell. If anything happened to him, though, she'd be dead, too, so he'd just have to put up with the frustration of being cautious.

As he slid the key into the lock and opened the door, he was recalling what she'd asked him. It seemed like weeks ago, but it had only been this morning.

After she'd shown him that picture of Turk, and he'd been trying to convince her she should go home, she'd said, "Have you ever let anyone get killed? Someone you were protecting, I mean?"

He hadn't. And he sure didn't intend to let her be the first. If she ended up dead he'd never forgive himself, because…

Oh, man, he didn't even want to think about the *because*. Somehow, for whatever crazy reason, he'd started to really care about her.

He closed the door and headed for the stairs, asking himself how stupid could he be?

He was her ticket to a front-page story. Her escape from Arts and Entertainment. Period.

Well, maybe not *period*. He knew he wasn't imagining the chemistry between them. But there was no way she'd want a man like him in her life. A man who was never in one place long enough to change a lightbulb.

Besides, he had no interest in changing lightbulbs. Or in anything else that went with a boring, routine existence.

Never had. Never would.

He reached the door of their room and knocked, quietly saying, "It's me."

When she opened up, she was still wearing her dress but her feet were bare.

He definitely didn't have a thing for feet, but hers struck him as extremely sexy.

Then she smiled at him and he suddenly felt a little less certain about the "never would."

And that scared the hell out of him.

"SEE...ANYONE OUT THERE?" Mickey asked after Dan locked the door of their room and turned toward her.

He shook his head, which was exactly what she'd been expecting. She figured that if he'd spotted anyone who even might have been Turk, he'd have said so right away.

But she wanted to tell him about her idea, and asking had seemed like a good way to lead into the subject.

She waited while he shrugged out of his jacket and set his gun down. Then, before she had a chance to say anything, he said, "I know it's not late but it's been a long couple of days. Do you think we should turn in?"

She glanced at the too-close-together beds, realizing she'd been concentrating so hard on her plan she'd almost forgotten about having to spend another night with him. Now that he'd reminded her, though, she could feel her blood getting hotter.

Telling herself she was simply going to ignore

whatever tricks her hormones played, she said, "There's something I'd like to talk about first."

"Sure."

When he sank onto one of the beds, she sat down facing him, careful not to let her knees touch his.

"So?" he said.

She hesitated, knowing he wasn't going to like the idea. Actually, she didn't like it herself, but since it was the only one she'd come up with she might as well get started.

"You said we have to get Turk," she reminded him.

"We will, Mickey."

"How?"

He simply studied her, which started her blood temperature slithering up another few degrees.

His eyes were saying that he knew how frightened she was. And that he'd give a lot if he could magically make things better for her.

She'd never before had a man look at her in quite that way, and it made her feel awfully glad she wasn't in this mess alone. That she had him to rely on. That he cared.

Exhaling slowly, she wondered how, in such a short time, they could possibly have gone from being strangers to where they were now. To having developed a connection that she wished could last. And maybe even turn into something....

She tried to keep the word *permanent* from forming in her head.

When that proved impossible, she told herself that

wanting something you knew you couldn't have was a fool's game. So she shouldn't be playing it.

She'd come to New York to get her story. Once she had it—assuming that was the way this all turned out—she'd be going home. While he'd be going heaven only knew where.

"I'm not sure exactly how we'll get him," he said at last. "Not yet. But there'll be a way. I won't let him hurt you."

"Promise?"

Although she'd meant that to be humorous, it came out sounding as if she was scared half to death.

Feeling stupid, she broke eye contact with Dan and looked at the floor.

"Hey," he said softly. "I'm a security specialist. Remember?"

She nodded, then told herself to finish what she'd started and said, "While you were gone, I thought of a way we might be able to trick him."

"Oh?"

He stared at her, and this time there was so much emotion in his eyes that she felt her throat begin to tighten.

Forcing her mind back to their problem, she said, "If I wasn't with you, I mean, if he thought I was alone but you were actually nearby, watching, he'd figure it would be easier to..."

She stopped speaking because Dan was shaking his head.

"No," he said. "We're not using you as bait."

"But if you were close by, and if—"

"No," he repeated more firmly. "You're in enough danger already. We're not doing anything that would heighten the risk."

She swallowed hard, all at once close to tears.

"Mickey?" he said softly.

When one of the damned tears spilled over, he moved to sit beside her and wrapped his arm around her shoulders.

Leaning against him, she simply sat breathing in his scent. She couldn't think what it reminded her of, but it was uniquely his, and as intoxicating as the aroma of the smoky Scotch that her father liked.

"Everything's going to be just fine," Dan murmured, drawing her even closer, his solid warmth so reassuring that she was almost able to believe his words.

But Daniel O'Neill wasn't superhuman. Or a magician. He was only a man.

A man she wanted and couldn't have.

That thought snuck up to bite her again, and she felt a few more tears trickling down her cheeks.

"Oh, Mickey," he whispered, wiping them away.

Then his lips were tentatively brushing hers, and that was all it took to undo every bit of her resolve.

She wrapped her arms around his neck and he kissed her, his mouth first hard against hers, then gentle as he nibbled at the hollow of her throat.

His hair tickled her jaw, and when she ran her fingers through it she remembered it was far too short.

Funny, but somewhere along the way she'd

stopped noticing that—just as she'd stopped noticing everything else she'd initially thought was wrong with him.

As she smoothed her hands down his back, he began grazing his knuckles against the bare skin of her leg, his touch sending such a hot craving through her that she moaned.

He kicked off his shoes then eased her down onto the bed, his hands moving to her breasts and his legs entwined with hers.

She could feel her desire becoming need, the need becoming urgent. Then he rolled over, pulling her with him so that she was lying on top of him with her hair cascading over his shoulders.

He brushed it back, framing her face in his hands, and resumed kissing her, more deeply this time, making her want him so badly that she reached down and stroked his erection.

"Jeez, Mickey," he whispered. "Don't do that unless you mean it."

"I mean it," she whispered back, wondering how he could have thought she might not.

He found the zipper on her dress and pulled it down, then helped her out of it.

When he removed her bra she felt…exposed. Vulnerable. But only until he began kissing her breasts, teasing her nipples with his tongue.

Then she felt nothing but such a sweet pain of longing that she wanted him inside her more than she'd ever wanted anything.

He left her for a moment. She watched in the fading light while he took a condom from his wallet and quickly removed his clothes.

Her gaze caressed the muscles of his shoulders and chest, his flat stomach, his hard penis—and her desire grew even more intense.

Snuggling down beside her again, he ran his hand possessively up her thigh and slid it beneath the elastic of her panties.

Every bit of air seemed to vanish from her lungs as he began touching her, teasing her, his fingers almost but not quite inside her, making her squirm against his touch, wordlessly begging him for more.

By the time he disposed of her panties, she was breathing in quick little gasps. And when he began kissing his way from her breasts to her waist, she thought she was going to melt from the inside out.

She grew positive of it when he continued lower. Melting was the only possible outcome when she felt this hot and wet.

"Oh, Dan," she murmured, so close to climaxing that she could say nothing more.

As desperately as she wanted release, she just as desperately wanted the exquisite aching to continue. Then a rush of spasms seized her, finally subsiding and leaving her so spent she couldn't have put two coherent words together.

Then Dan was inside her and she was climaxing again. She clung to him, certain it was the only thing that would keep her from shattering into a million pieces. Finally she felt him shudder, and her own release followed a second later.

After that, for a minute—or ten—they simply lay together, breathing hard, the air cool against their damp skin.

Finally, he eased off her and cuddled her closely to him. Close enough that she could hear his heart, still beating fast, and could feel the warmth of his breath against her shoulder.

Lying beside him like this brought her the nearest she'd ever come to a sense of perfection, and when reality began tiptoeing around in her head, trying to remind her of a dozen different things she didn't want to think about, she ordered it to leave her alone.

Since she knew there wouldn't be any future for her with Dan, she intended to relish every second of the present.

DAN WOKE UP to the aroma of coffee and fresh baking wafting up from the main floor of the B and B—and to the warmth of Mickey beside him.

It made him feel… Man, oh, man, he couldn't think of the words to describe how good it made him feel.

He could still remember the time when he was a little kid, only three or four, when a thunderstorm had rolled noisily through New Orleans, sending him scurrying across the room to spend the night in the safety of his big brother's bed.

The following morning was the last time he hadn't woken up alone in bed. Until today.

He looked at Mickey again. Well, no, that wasn't accurate. He could hardly be looking at her *again* when he hadn't taken his eyes off her since the moment he'd opened them.

She was still asleep, curled up naked against him, and he was barely breathing so that he wouldn't wake her before he'd had time to think.

He'd always made a point of not spending an entire night with a woman, even if he liked her a lot, because he'd never wanted to find himself falling into the habit of...

Well, he'd never wanted to give anyone the impression that he was more serious than he actually was.

But, hell, why he'd done it didn't matter in the least. What mattered was that falling asleep with Mickey in his arms had felt so good he wouldn't have gotten up and moved to the other bed for all the money in the world.

He glanced at the bedside clock, thinking that making love for half the night, on top of his lack of sleep over the past few days, had really put him out for the count.

It was late enough that they should already be up and on their way, yet he didn't have the heart to disturb her.

Or was the truth that he simply wanted to lie here with her for a little longer?

He suspected that was it, because waking up with her next to him, all soft and warm, had started him remembering—in incredible detail—just how terrific last night had been.

Hell, it had been so amazing that he seriously wished she didn't live way out on the West Coast.

Of course, if he told the RCI people he'd be really interested in any assignments that came up in California...

But that got him back to thinking that Mickey just wasn't the type of woman who'd be content with a part-time man.

And when had he started even toying with the idea that he might like to be someone's part-time man?

Before he came up with the answer, Mickey made a tiny noise. Then she sleepily opened her eyes and gave him the sexiest smile he'd seen in his entire life.

It made him want so badly to start back in where they'd left off a few hours ago that he could hardly keep from doing exactly that.

''Morning,'' she murmured.

''Morning.''

He risked propping himself up on his elbow and giving her a lingering kiss. But when she began to run a fingernail down his chest, he reluctantly grabbed her hand and said, ''Hold that thought till later.''

''Why?''

'''Cuz if we don't get out of this bed now, we're going to end up here all day. And we've got places to go. People to see.''

''You're right,'' she said with a little sigh.

And like it or not, he knew he was.

The world hadn't stopped turning and Turk was still out there—a threat not only to Billy's life, but to Mickey's and his.

CHAPTER FIFTEEN

DAN STOOD STARING OUT at the activity on lower Broadway and doing his best to be patient.

After a quick breakfast, he'd wanted to head directly to see Billy's former agent. However, he could hardly have argued about making this one stop. Not after Mickey had pointed out that whenever "the story finally broke," as she'd put it, she absolutely had to have a camera with her.

Besides, she was buying a twin of the one Turk had stolen, which meant she wouldn't have to go over its special features with the clerk or anything. It was basically just a matter of getting the sale processed.

He glanced over toward the counter, thinking that for such a straightforward transaction it was taking an awfully long time. And the store, with its big front window, had him feeling as if he was in a damn goldfish bowl.

Anyone outside could easily see in. So if Turk had grown tired of just following them, if he'd decided...well, the saying might be *like shooting fish in a barrel,* but shooting them in a goldfish bowl wouldn't be any harder.

Telling himself that worrying never did any good, he had another look outside, once again making sure that their taxi was still waiting for them.

As much as he disliked relying on cabs, it hadn't made sense to use the rental this morning. Hector Washington's agency was on West Forty-seventh, and both the traffic and the parking in the theater district were ridiculous.

Besides, being dropped off at the door was distinctly safer than having to walk from a parking lot.

On that thought, he let his gaze drift slowly along the block. He still didn't see the slightest sign of the hit man, but that did nothing to improve his state of mind. In fact, it only made him more concerned about just how good their killer was. Because he might not have managed to spot Turk yet, but he still could feel the man's presence in his bones.

It was like sensing that the angel of death was following them, except that Turk was no angel. And knowing he had them in his sights but not being able to do much about it was frustrating as hell.

If Dan had been on his own, he'd have dug into his bag of tricks and found one that would draw the guy into view, which got him back to the problem of having to be more cautious than usual because of Mickey.

Since every last one of those tricks involved risk, the only thing he could do was what he was already doing—keep constantly vigilant.

That, however, didn't feel like nearly enough.

He glanced in Mickey's direction once more, just

as she turned from the counter and started toward him, a new camera bag slung over her shoulder.

"Get everything you need?" he asked, trying to sound as if he didn't have a care in the world.

"Uh-huh. And thanks. I know you could have done without the shopping."

"No problem," he lied.

Once they were back in the relative safety of the cab, and on their way uptown, she said, "You know, before we meet this Hector Washington, you should probably tell me why he's suing Billy."

"Didn't I explain yesterday?" he said, checking that the Plexiglas divider behind the driver was tightly shut.

Discussing Billy's business with Mickey was one thing; having a stranger overhear was another.

"Not really," she was saying. "Not in any detail, I mean. You basically just said that Billy figures Washington might rather see him dead than in court."

"Oh. Well, the suit's pretty straightforward. When Billy signed on with his current agency, he didn't terminate his contract with Washington even though he was obliged to under its provisions."

"Why not?"

Dan shrugged. "Just didn't bother. The parting was anything but amicable, so maybe that was a factor. And Billy's not a detail person at the best of times. But the point is, the contract with Washington was legally still in effect when the new agent put together Billy's initial movie deal."

"Which was for his first three films."

He looked at her, surprised she knew that.

"I was supposed to interview Billy, remember?" she said. "I read up on his career."

"Oh. Right. Well, at any rate, Washington's claim is that he's entitled to the representation fees for those three movies. That amounts to a potful of money."

"I'll bet. And has he got a strong case?"

"Uh-huh. Apparently it's practically open-and-shut. The contract clearly stated that he had an ongoing entitlement."

"Then if he's bound to win anyway, why would he bother trying to kill Billy?"

"Well, keep in mind that the idea he might is *Billy's* theory."

"But you figured it made enough sense to put him on your shortlist."

He nodded. "There were a couple of things that added up neatly. First off, Billy's lawyers have been dragging out the pretrial stuff and it's costing Washington a lot of money.

"And second, whether Billy's a nice guy or not, he's a hell of an actor. So Washington could be worried that he's good enough to convince a judge he merely made an innocent mistake. An oversight. If he managed that, he might not have to pay Washington as much. But if Billy couldn't testify because he was dead..."

"Ah," Mickey murmured. "Then Washington would be a shoo-in to get the whole potful."

"Exactly," he said as the cabbie turned onto West Forty-seventh.

Their destination, near Times Square and practically beside the Ethel Barrymore Theater, proved to be one of those decrepit old buildings whose owners charged outrageous rents based solely on location.

As the driver pulled up at the curb, Dan said, "Would you mind waiting again?"

"Sorry, but I'm going off shift."

Telling himself there'd be no problem hailing a taxi in this neighborhood, Dan paid the man and climbed out, carefully surveying the street as Mickey followed him.

There was no sign of Turk, but he could easily be in another taxi. Or lurking in his car, waiting to see exactly where they were going.

As he headed up the narrow stairway with Mickey, he said, "Just follow my lead again. That worked perfectly with the Brents."

When she smiled, clearly pleased, he found himself wanting to kiss her right there on the stairs. But he had to stop letting distracting thoughts like that mess with his mind. One slip, one lapse of attention, could get them killed.

"Just what am I supposed to be watching for with Mr. Washington?" Mickey said as they started along the third-floor hallway.

"Oh, shifty eyes. Perspiration. Anxious body language. Nervousness in his voice. All the standard stuff. And what he actually says, of course."

When they reached the Hector Washington

Agency, Dan was surprised that the place wasn't bigger.

Billy had referred to it as small, but "one man show" was probably a more accurate description.

Or one man and a receptionist, to be precise.

Small or not, though, as soon as they got there it was clear they were in luck. The door to the single office off the reception area was standing half-open, and a man in his early sixties was inside talking on the phone.

Billy had described Washington as fat, bald and ugly, and since this guy looked like a grizzled bulldog he had to be their man.

The young woman sitting at a desk glanced at them as if they were a most unwelcome intrusion, and said, "Yes?"

"We'd like to see Mr. Washington," Dan told her. "My name is O'Neill."

She looked at her book, as if she actually thought she might find his name penciled in, then shook her head.

"I'm sorry, but Mr. Washington is very busy today. If you'd like to set something up for another time—"

"No, it's important we speak to him right away. As soon as he's finished his call."

"I'm afraid he has someone with an appointment coming in shortly, but as I was saying—"

"Tell him it's regarding Billy Brent," Dan interrupted, setting a business card down in front of her.

"Oh," she said, obviously taken aback when she heard Billy's name.

"Well, if you won't need much time..."

He smiled. "Almost none."

"Then I'm sure he'll see you."

A couple of minutes later, once Hector Washington had hung up the phone, the receptionist scurried into his office with Dan's card. Thirty seconds after that, Washington was on his feet, warily inviting them in.

As the receptionist closed the door on her way out, Dan extended his hand, saying, "Daniel O'Neill. And this is Mickey Westover."

Washington eyed the camera bag curiously.

Mickey said, "I don't like to leave things in the car. You know."

He nodded, then turned his attention back to Dan. "I understand you're here about Billy Brent."

"That's right."

"Well, my lawyer's advised me not to discuss the lawsuit with anyone, so if it's about that—"

"It's not."

Washington slowly gestured toward the two visitors' chairs and sat back down behind his desk, looking no less suspicious.

"Personal security advisor," he said, eyeing Dan's card for a moment, then waiting to see where his visitors would go from there.

"Uh-huh," Dan said. "And right now I'm working for Billy. Because someone's put a contract on his life."

"You're serious?"

Dan nodded.

"Sonofabitch," Washington muttered, almost under his breath. "So the jerk finally pissed someone off too much," he added. "And you're here because?"

"We thought you might have some idea of who it could be."

The agent leaned back in his chair. "You mean you think it might be me."

Dan gave him a few beats, just in case he wanted to either deny or confirm that it *was* him.

Then, in the face of Washington's silence, he said, "We're talking to a lot of people, not just you. A lot of people who know Billy well. Who know his associates and friends."

"Look, I knew Billy well. Past tense. And I damned well might have paid for a contract on the slimy bastard at one time."

He glanced at Mickey for long enough to say "Pardon my French," then looked at Dan again and said, "But that time was years ago. As for his associates, I wouldn't know his current associates if I bumped into them on the street. And when it comes to friends, unless things have changed he doesn't have any.

"If you want to talk enemies, that's a different story. I could give you enough names to fill the Manhattan phone book. It would be a pretty stale list, though. I haven't seen Billy Brent in over five years. And I'd be happy to go another fifty without seeing him. But regardless of that, as I said, my lawyer advised me not to discuss the lawsuit. And I'm sure he'd say the same thing about this subject. So our meeting's over."

"NOT EXACTLY a Billy Brent fan," Mickey said once Dan had closed the door and they were heading down the hallway outside Washington's agency.

The smile he gave her looked forced, so she added, "You're disappointed, aren't you. Because you don't know whether to leave him on the list or not."

"Got it in one. What was your take?"

"I'm not sure either. But I almost choked when he said he might have been willing to pay for a contract on Billy. I mean, even though he was talking years ago, my first thought was that he'd never have said that if he'd hired Turk.

"But then I started thinking about reverse psychology, and wondering whether he was just acting the way he was because he figured we wouldn't expect a guilty man to behave like that.

"On the other hand," she continued, "if he *is* behind the contract...well, wouldn't most people have been a lot more pleasant? Made an effort to seem cooperative? To throw us off track? Is that sounding like garble or am I making any sense?" she added as they started down the stairs.

"Yeah, you're making sense," Dan said. "And you're pretty much where I am. Without knowing more about him, we can't tell what game he's playing. Or if he's playing one at all.

"Maybe he's just the sort of guy who says whatever he wants and could care less what people think."

Mickey took a few stairs in silence—disheartened that they didn't seem to be getting anywhere—before she said, "So we didn't completely eliminate June Brent, and we're certainly not eliminating Washington. And we haven't even gotten to the ex-girlfriend. The only one we've ruled out is Cole, and an eighteen-year-old didn't really seem too likely from the start."

Dan looked at her, not even attempting a smile this time. "You sound as if you're feeling a little discouraged."

"You can leave out the *little.* Detective stuff is a lot harder in real life than on TV."

"Well, maybe things will improve when we talk to Maria Rosemount."

"Let's hope," she said.

Once they reached the street, she uneasily watched the way Dan kept a close eye on the surrounding area while trying to flag down a taxi.

Before they'd left the B and B, he'd told her to stay alert because Turk might still be following them.

But she had to think that "might" had only been an attempt to lower her worry level a little, because last night he'd said that they had to assume Turk was definitely still keeping them under surveillance.

And nothing had changed since last night.

They knew Turk was out to kill Billy. And they knew what he looked like. Which meant they were as much a threat to him today as they'd been yesterday.

The longer she thought about that the more nervous she got, and when a cabbie wheeled through two lanes of traffic and pulled up beside them, she felt a serious rush of relief.

Dan gave the man an address on the Upper West Side and they started off, with Dan staring through the rear window.

When he finally shifted around, she knew he hadn't seen Turk. But she also knew that didn't mean anything.

Deciding that talking would get her mind off their killer, she said, ''Do you think this Maria will be home?''

''Hopefully. She doesn't work.''

''No?''

Dan leaned forward and slid the cab's divider shut before he said, ''She used to help design stage sets. That was how Billy met her. But he pays enough in child support to let her stay home with their daughter.''

''Well, at least he's not stingy, but you know...''

''What?''

She shrugged. ''This has absolutely nothing to do with the contract. I was just remembering what you said yesterday about Cole basically being able to get as much money as he wants from his father. That obviously hasn't made him a happy kid. And I wonder what growing up will be like for this little girl. Do you know her name?''

''Kathryn.''

''And you said she's five?''

''Uh-huh.''

''Does Billy ever see her, or does he just send checks?''

''He told me he visits her now and then. If he's in New York and has some time.

''But that was pretty much all he said about their relationship. Mostly, we discussed Maria.''

''Some relationship,'' she muttered.

When Dan let that pass with just a shrug, she said, ''So what made you put Maria on the shortlist?''

''Well, for starters, I figure she might hate Billy's guts.''

''Really? I thought you said she has no hard feelings.''

''I think what I said is she *claims* not to. But even though Billy seems to believe that…''

''You don't?''

''I've got my doubts.

''See, it was while Maria was pregnant that he decided he was heading for Hollywood. And when he told her about it, and said June would be staying in New York, Maria assumed that meant he was going to marry her.''

''You heard this from him?''

''Uh-huh. At any rate, when it turned out that wasn't the deal, that he wasn't even asking her to go with him, let alone suggesting marriage, she was…''

''Devastated? And furious?'' Mickey guessed, trying to imagine how *she'd* feel if she was pregnant and getting dumped.

"Yeah, both of those are probably good words. But according to Billy, she came around when she realized he didn't intend to leave her wanting financially."

"You think she might not have, though. Not really."

"Right. I figure that maybe she only convinced him she had so he wouldn't change his mind about the generous support payments. But regardless of that, he's never disputed that he's Kathryn's father. So if he died she'd be entitled to part of his estate."

"By law, you're saying. Whether she's named in the will or not."

"Uh-huh. And I'm sure Maria must be aware of that.

"It's not really relevant, though, because Kathryn *is* named as a beneficiary. There's a dollar amount specified for her, and if Billy died she'd be an extremely wealthy little girl."

"Oh? And is Maria aware of that?"

"Billy says no, that he's never said a word to her about the will."

"But you think she might have found out what's in it?"

"I think it's possible. I don't know how, but it's the main reason she's on my shortlist."

Mickey considered this latest revelation, then her thoughts wandered back to the question of what Kathryn's growing-up years would be like.

She certainly hoped Maria was a good mother.

"What are you thinking about now?" Dan said.

"Oh, just wondering if Billy ever considers other people. I mean, how could he have a daughter and only see her if he happens to be in New York and has nothing better to do for a couple of hours?"

When Dan didn't reply, she added, "You know, with four kids, my folks didn't have a lot of spare money. But I never cared much, and I know my brothers didn't either. Our parents were always there for us, and that's what was important. If one of my brothers had a wrestling match or was playing football, they'd be watching. And my dad must have spent a million hours helping me with my high school chemistry. I was so hopeless that I'd never have graduated without him."

There was another silence before Dan said, "Not all families are like yours."

"I know. But people shouldn't have children unless they're prepared to put time and effort into raising them."

"Yeah, well, it happens."

Suddenly, it struck her that he must be thinking about his own family—about the mother he'd said had died a while back, the father he'd never been close to and the brother in prison.

She rested her hand on his, and when he looked at her, she said, "Can I ask you something?"

"Sure."

"What were your parents like when you were a boy?"

He hesitated before saying, ''I thought you meant to ask me something more about Billy.''

''No. I was wondering about you.''

He shrugged, looking uncomfortable.

''My folks were always busy,'' he told her at last. ''My mom was a waitress and she was gone most nights. By the time Sean and I got home from school, she'd be ready to leave.''

''And your dad?''

''He'd be there to give us supper. At least, he was there when I was really little. After Sean got old enough to make sandwiches, the old man would usually stop off after work for a few beers. And by the time he finally rolled in, the smartest thing we could do was just stay out of his way.

''Sean actually did a lot more to bring me up than my parents. I really owe him.''

''Oh, Dan,'' she said softly.

In her house, dinner had been family time, and there'd rarely been anyone absent from the table.

''It's no big deal,'' he was saying. ''I survived.''

''I know, but...''

''But what?''

''You missed so much.''

He shrugged. ''What's the old saying? You can't miss what you never had?''

She wanted to wrap her arms around him and hold him tight.

The back seat of a cab was hardly the place, though, so she simply stared out the window, not certain what to say next.

“And your brother?” she asked at last.

“What about him?”

“You told me he was in San Quentin, and I was just wondering if you keep in touch.”

“As well as I can.”

“And with your father?”

“No.”

No. One word. Spoken quickly and firmly.

He might as well have come right out and told her not to ask anything more on that topic.

“This is the street,” he said as the cabbie turned onto West Seventy-third. “Now we just have to hope Maria is home.”

CHAPTER SIXTEEN

WHERE THE UPPER EAST SIDE virtually screamed, *Money,* the ritzy enclaves of the Upper West Side merely whispered it. But the brownstone that Maria Rosemount and Billy's daughter occupied, one in a row of attached brick dwellings, was a lovely old place.

Originally, Dan thought, it had probably been a single family home. Now the trio of buzzers beside the entrance told him that each of the three stories was a separate apartment.

M. Rosemount, he saw, glancing at the names, lived on the ground floor.

While Mickey peered through the little window in the center of the door—protected by miniatures of the wrought iron bars that encased all the main floor windows—he turned toward the street and did a final check up and down the block, making sure their invisible killer hadn't chosen this moment to materialize.

When he turned back, Mickey gestured for him to have a look inside.

The walls of the small but elegant foyer boasted

mahogany wainscoting and an Oriental carpet large enough to cover most of the floor.

A polished wooden staircase ran along the wall on one side, opposite the entrance to the first-floor apartment.

"Nice," he said, stepping back from the door and pressing the top buzzer.

"That's not hers," Mickey pointed out.

"I know. I want to see whether the neighbors are home."

"Why?"

"You never know what might turn out to be useful information."

When there was no response, he tried the middle buzzer.

"Let's hope Maria's not out, too," Mickey said after another minute of dead air.

He pushed the buzzer beside her name, and almost immediately saw a curtain move at the window nearest the steps. Maria, he assumed, was giving them the once-over.

"Yes?" a disembodied woman's voice said a few seconds later.

"Maria Rosemount?" he said into the intercom.

"Yes?"

"My name is Daniel O'Neill. Billy Brent asked me to come and talk with you."

There was a tiny silence before Maria said, "He didn't tell me to expect anyone."

"No, he didn't have a chance. But it's essential

that I see you. He has a problem and you might be able to help him.''

''Well, of course, I'll try. But this is a really bad time. Could you come back in an hour or so?''

''It would be better if we had a few minutes now.''

''I'm sorry, but...make it *half* an hour.''

''Sure,'' he said. ''My associate and I will just wait, though. And would you mind letting us into the foyer? It's awfully hot out here in the sun.''

This time the silence lasted much longer, but the lock buzzer finally sounded.

Dan opened the door and ushered Mickey inside.

''We're going to stand in here for half an hour?'' she whispered as he closed the door.

''If that's how long it takes.''

''But there was a coffee shop down on the corner. We could—''

''No, we'll stay here.''

''Because?''

''Why,'' he said, lowering his voice, ''do you think she didn't want us to come right in?''

''I don't know. Maybe her place is a mess. Or she's a mess. Or Kathryn's in the middle of a temper tantrum.''

''Uh-huh, it could be any of those things. Or it might be that she has a man in there. And she'd rather Billy didn't find out.''

''Would he care?''

''Probably.''

''Really?''

''Well, you can never be sure what Billy's take on

anything will be, but I doubt he'd like her having a boyfriend. And she probably worries that if she does anything to tick him off he'll rethink his generosity to her."

"But the idea of him caring whether she has a boyfriend is ridiculous. Isn't it? I mean, she *is* history, isn't she?"

"As far as I know. But the way Billy thinks about a lot of things is pretty strange. At any rate, if there is someone in there with her I'd like to know who it is."

"Why?"

"Because she's on my shortlist."

Mickey seemed ready to ask *why?* again, and he hoped she wouldn't.

He didn't feel like getting into an explanation about how, in his line of work, anybody you crossed paths with could be the one who held the key you needed.

Thankfully, all she said was, "Well, if there is someone, and she doesn't want you to know that, won't she just sneak him out the back way?"

"There isn't one. The backs of these buildings are practically joined to the ones on the next street. The only way out is through the front. Or from the basement. There's usually a door under the front steps.

"But that's the way to the basement," he added, pointing to the wooden door built into the side of the staircase. "So someone would have to walk right past us to get there."

"Ah," Mickey said.

MARIA ROSEMOUNT DIDN'T actually make Mickey and Dan wait half an hour. She opened her apartment door after only a few minutes and politely invited them inside.

She was a willowy brunette, and so gorgeous that Mickey glanced at Dan to check his reaction to her.

He didn't appear to be having one, something she found enormously pleasing. After last night, if she'd caught him drooling at the mere sight of another woman...

As the three of them did the introductions thing, she told herself that her feeling possessive of Dan was as ridiculous as Billy feeling possessive of Maria. Because, regardless of last night, Daniel O'Neill was not going to be a permanent fixture in her life.

She did her best to ignore the sharp pang the thought caused, and when Maria's gaze lingered on the camera bag, she trotted out her "don't like to leave things in the car" line again.

Then, as they stepped into the living room, she glanced around to see if she could spot any sign of other company.

She couldn't. It was a large apartment, though, with a hall stretching off the living room.

"I'm sorry to have kept you waiting," Maria said, gesturing them to sit on the couch. "But I was just putting my daughter down for her nap, and company gets her all wound up."

As Dan said "No problem," Mickey wondered why, if it was nap time, Maria had Diana Krall turned up loudly.

"So," Maria said. "Billy sent you."

Dan nodded, then launched straight into the hit man story—just giving her a bare-bones summary, not going into any details about knowing who the hit man was, let alone mentioning that they'd had a couple of encounters with him.

Unlike June Brent and Hector Washington, Maria seemed horrified to hear that Billy's life was in danger.

"What can I do to help?" she asked when Dan was through.

"Well, because you're in regular contact with Billy, we're hoping you might have some idea of who could be behind this."

Maria gazed at him for a long moment before saying, "Did Billy tell you we're in *regular* contact?"

"You're one of the people he suggested I talk to."

"I don't know why," she said, looking puzzled. "I mean, if I had any ideas I'd certainly share them, but I'm not really up on what goes on in Billy's life these days. I only see him two or three times a year. Only when he comes to visit our daughter. And even then we don't talk much. In fact, I generally go out so that Kathryn can have him all to herself. She sees very little of him and…well, the point is, aside from being Kathryn's mother, I'm not part of Billy's life anymore. I really don't understand why he'd have thought I'd be any help at all.

"I wish I could be, but…" Maria shrugged and left it at that.

"He's never mentioned anything about having a problem with someone?" Dan tried.

"How well do you know Billy?" she asked.

"Not too well. Why?"

"Because he's a dear, sweet man. But he's always having a problem with someone. Actually, at any given time, he's usually having problems with a dozen different people. That's just the way he is. When we were together, I learned to simply tune him out when he got going about one of them. But that was long ago. And I'm sure he's had ten thousand problem people in his life since then. In any event, I'm sorry he's in such serious trouble and I wish I could help. Please tell him that."

Maria rose from the couch, giving a clear message that she'd like them to leave.

"Do you think I could use your bathroom before we go?" Mickey asked.

Maybe, if she got out of Maria's sight, she could see what there was to see. Or *who* there was to see, as the case might be.

"Of course," Maria said. "It's this way."

Mickey followed along down the hall, wishing she had X-ray vision. Aside from the kitchen, the door to every room was closed.

"Here we are," Maria said, opening the door to reveal a luxuriously renovated bathroom.

"Thanks. I'll just be a minute."

She stepped inside and closed the door, then pressed her ear against it.

If Maria was walking back to the living room, she was doing it in total silence.

After a minute or so, she flushed and ran the tap.

When she quietly opened the door, Maria was standing mere feet away, her fingers resting on the edges of one of the framed prints that hung along the hall.

She flashed a smile and said, "I don't know how these pictures get crooked but they always seem to need straightening. Sometimes, I think this apartment must be haunted."

Mickey forced herself to smile back.

Obviously she could do with more practice in the detecting department.

"DON'T WORRY ABOUT IT," Dan told Mickey as they headed down the street.

"But if I could have gotten a better look around we'd have known whether—"

"We do know," he interrupted.

"You're sure?"

"Uh-huh."

"And you're sure because?"

He did another quick check that there was still nothing suspicious in the vicinity, then said, "In the first place, she was nervous."

"I didn't notice that."

"Trust me—she was. Second, you were right about the music. There's no way it would have been that loud if she'd really put the kid down to nap. She had it turned up so we wouldn't hear if Kathryn started talking to someone. And third, why the hell would she have stood in the hall waiting for you unless she was worried that you might do a little snooping?''

He glanced back toward Maria's place, decided there was no way they could still be seen from it and stopped walking.

''What do we do now?'' Mickey asked.

''We wait until he comes out. Then we follow him and see if he goes anywhere interesting.''

''You're really positive that someone's in there.''

He nodded. ''I get gut feelings about this sort of thing, and I've got a really strong one right now. But we can't stand out here in the middle of the street while we're waiting.

''I wish we had the car,'' he added.

''It made more sense to take cabs,'' Mickey reminded him.

''Right. *Made.* Past tense, as Hector Washington would say.''

He dug his cellular from his pocket and punched in Lydia's number at RCI.

''Lydia, it's Dan,'' he said when she answered. ''Sorry to bother you for something stupid, but I need a cab and I don't have a phone book.''

''You're still in Manhattan?''

''Uh-huh.''

''Give me a couple of seconds.''

He waited, visualizing her pulling the information up on her computer screen.

''Okay, here you are.''

As she rattled off a number, he filed it into his short-term memory. After he'd thanked her and clicked off, he called it.

''Are we going to sit in the cab until our guy comes out?'' Mickey asked when he was done speaking with the dispatcher.

''Uh-huh.''

''Then let's hope he's not spending the night.''

''THIS IS GETTING AWFULLY TIRED, awfully fast, isn't it?'' Dan said.

When Mickey nodded, he reached for her hand and gave it an encouraging squeeze.

All he had to do was look at her and he literally had to touch her. It made him wonder just how much he'd miss her when she went home and he moved on to his next assignment.

He had a horrible suspicion it was going to be a hell of a lot, and that was not how things were supposed to have played out.

He risked glancing at her again, and this time it made him want to kiss her, so he forced his gaze from her and looked through the Plexiglas barrier at the back of the cabbie's head.

For a substantial bonus on top of his ''standing'' rate, the man had agreed to turn the engine on and run the air conditioner every few minutes, which meant that at least they weren't sweltering. But that was the most positive thing he could say about sitting here.

It was boring as hell. And given their particular circumstances, it was far from safe.

Turk still had them under surveillance. Dan would have bet serious money on that. And sooner or later, the man would make a move. So if there was any other way of insuring that Maria's company didn't slip off unnoticed…

But there wasn't, which meant they had to hang in.

He just wished the phrase *drive-by shooting* would stop wandering around in his mind.

While he was scanning the street yet again, and telling himself—for about the millionth time—that as long as he stayed alert they should be okay, his phone began ringing.

"Daniel O'Neill," he answered it.

There was no response for long enough that he almost clicked off before his caller said, "Dan, it's your father."

The moment he heard Patrick O'Neill's voice, he could feel his heartbeat accelerating.

And when Mickey whispered "What's wrong?" he realized that his face must have lost a shade or two of color.

"Dan?" his father said.

"Yes. I'm here."

"Well. It's been a while, hasn't it."

"Uh-huh. It has."

His father cleared his throat, then said, "I'm calling about your brother."

Oh, man, something had happened to Sean!

"He's getting out."

As the words sank in, he could feel relief seeping through his veins.

"They're giving him early parole, and I thought..."

"What?"

"Well, he won't be able to leave California. Not as long as he's on parole, I mean."

"Right."

"So I thought...well, I told him I'd go out there. Spend a few days with him. And since I haven't seen either of you since your mother's funeral, I wondered if maybe..."

He swallowed hard, knowing where this was going and not sure how he wanted to handle it.

"If maybe what?" he said at last.

"Well...if you could take a little time off and we could go together."

"I..."

"If you can't, I understand," his father said quickly. "I only thought..."

"Dan?" Mickey whispered.

When he glanced at her, she had her camera out of its case and was attaching a telephoto lens to it.

Without stopping what she was doing, she nodded in the direction of Maria's place.

He looked along toward it and saw that a man was standing on the front steps saying goodbye to Maria.

Somewhere in his early thirties, he was tall, slim and casually dressed.

"There's something going on here," Dan said into

the phone while Mickey opened her window and aimed the camera.

"But I'll call you back," he added, as the man started down the steps and Mickey began clicking off shots.

"Sure," Patrick said before hanging up.

Dan tapped on the divider, and when the cabbie slid it open he said, "That's him."

The cabbie eyed the man for a few seconds before glancing at Dan and saying, "He got a gun?"

"I don't think so."

"Well, turns out he does, I don't follow him another inch."

"Fair enough," Dan said, wishing again that he hadn't decided to go with cabs today.

The three of them watched Maria's friend walk about a hundred feet, then stop and unlock a parked car.

"When he pulls out of his space," Dan told Mickey, "you should be able to read the plate with your telephoto."

As she focused her camera on the car, he said to the driver, "Try to stay back far enough that he won't notice us, but don't lose him."

Ten seconds later, Mickey said, "Okay, I've got the plate in focus."

She read off the number and Dan jotted it down, feeling a whole lot better.

It would take Lydia no time at all to learn who the owner of that car was. So now, even if they lost the guy, they'd have his name and address.

Unless, of course, it wasn't his car.

That was always a possibility, and a good reason for following him.

As they headed toward midtown, he called Lydia once more and gave her the number.

''Late model. Black. I think it's a Pontiac,'' he added without taking his eyes off it.

''And once you've got an ID on the guy, would you check the basics. Where he works, what he does, anything you can find out fast.''

His most recent gut feeling was telling him that this fellow just might be the one holding the key they needed.

''Dan?'' Mickey said after he'd finished talking to Lydia.

''Uh-huh?'' he said, his focus still on the car ahead of them.

''Who phoned before? You looked...almost shocked.''

Yeah. *Shocked* was a good word.

''Just a voice from the past,'' he said.

''Oh?''

He didn't let himself glance at her. He knew she was watching him, waiting for him to elaborate, and he didn't want to.

At least not until after he'd had a chance to sort out his thoughts.

And probably not even then.

''You aren't going to tell me who?'' she said at last.

''Later, okay?''

He gave her a smile and reached for her hand once more, hoping she'd forget about it but doubting he'd be that lucky.

They were driving down Park Avenue when Lydia phoned him back.

"There's a minor glitch," she said. "The car's leased, so the registration is in the leasing company's name. And its computer system is down. Until it's up and running again, there's no way of getting anything."

"But you'll keep on top of it."

"Really, Dan. How often have I let you down?"

"Never."

"Right," she said before hanging up.

"Problem?" Mickey asked.

"Only a temporary one."

As he was explaining, the black car turned off Park Avenue and onto a cross street.

The cabbie barely made it around the corner in time for them to see it pull into a parking garage.

"Now what?" he asked, looking back at Dan.

He thought rapidly.

He wanted to know where this fellow was going, but if he spotted the cab pulling into the garage after him he could well realize he was being followed.

On the other hand, there was no guarantee he'd come out through the pedestrian exit onto the street. He might use a different one.

Telling himself that it wouldn't be the end of the world if he did, that Lydia would come up with his name shortly, he dug his wallet from his pocket and said, "We'll get out here."

CHAPTER SEVENTEEN

FROM WHERE HE'D STOPPED, Turk eyed the two cops who were standing, talking, on the far side of the street. Then he focused on the cab again and watched it pull away, leaving O'Neill and the Westover woman behind.

For a couple of seconds, he let himself fantasize about putting a few bullets through her new camera bag, which, of course, would continue on through her. Then he'd take a shot or two at O'Neill.

However, that was only a fantasy, because this wasn't the good time and place he was waiting for. It wouldn't be, even without those cops.

Most people pretty much stopped thinking when they heard gunfire, but there was always the danger of someone catching your plate number. So if you were going to make your getaway in a car, it had better be a stolen one.

He turned his attention back to O'Neill and the reporter as they walked a little ways along the block and paused in front of a deli, looking as if they were thinking about going in.

Actually, he knew, they were just waiting for Jake Remmington to come out of the parkade.

He'd practically gone into cardiac arrest when he'd seen Remmington leaving Maria Rosemount's place. Them knowing each other put a whole different slant on this job, and it wasn't a slant that made him happy. Not at all.

Then, when the other two had taken off after Remmington...

Hell, it had been like a damn parade, with him following their cab while they followed Remmington's car. And he didn't enjoy parades.

At the moment, in fact, he wasn't enjoying anything.

This whole freaking job had gotten way too complicated for comfort, and if he hadn't already decided that he had to eliminate some of the players—fast—this new twist with Remmington would have convinced him of it.

Of course, when the man had come to him, he hadn't asked why he wanted Billy Brent dead. That simply wasn't protocol. But if he'd had even a clue that Remmington was mixed up with one of Billy's old girlfriends...

Well, he hadn't. And he didn't know exactly what the deal was between them. Whatever it was, though, it might well be another problem he didn't need. Especially not on top of what O'Neill and the woman were up to.

It hadn't occurred to him yesterday, when they'd visited June Brent. But today...

He did his research when he was planning a hit, which meant he knew who some of Billy's acquaintances were. And a little about his relationships with them.

So when those two had gone to see Hector Washington and then Maria Rosemount…

Dammit, the hope they might lead him to Billy had been nothing more than wishful thinking. They were too busy trying to determine who'd hired him. Figuring that if they could do that they could get to him.

It wasn't going to happen, though. Not unless Jake Remmington talked out of turn. Or had *already* talked out of turn.

He rubbed his jaw, feeling uneasy about Remmington. And that was unusual.

Normally he didn't worry much about any of his clients saying the wrong thing, because he'd only take a job if he knew for sure who was paying him.

Oh, some contract killers would deal with a middleman, but he always insisted on a face-to-face meeting. That way, he could make absolutely certain that whoever bought his services understood the law—knew that anyone who paid him to whack someone was as guilty as if he'd pulled the trigger himself—as far as the courts were concerned, at least.

Of course he always assured his clients he wouldn't get caught, which meant that nobody was going to end up charged with murder.

He didn't want to scare off business.

But it was important that they understood the rules. It guaranteed silence.

Still, there was always the risk that someone would slip up and say the wrong thing to the wrong people. Especially if the wrong people kept running all over town asking questions.

He looked across the street at O'Neill and the woman again, absently resting his hand on the butt of his gun.

Just as soon as he saw a good chance, it would be game over for those two.

"DO YOU THINK we've lost him?" Mickey asked Dan at last.

It was almost ten minutes since the black car had disappeared into the parking garage, which she assumed meant that Maria Rosemount's friend wouldn't be using the exit they were watching.

"Probably," Dan said. "Unless he's just sitting talking on his phone or something."

"Should we go in? See if we can spot him?"

He glanced slowly up and down the street, then shook his head.

She nervously did her own visual survey, and even though she saw no sign of Turk she was glad that Dan had vetoed her idea.

Everyone knew parkades weren't the safest places at the best of times.

"There's really nothing more we can do until Lydia calls," Dan said. "So why don't we have a quick lunch, then take a cab back to the bed-and-breakfast. That way, we'll have the car when we want it. I've had enough of taxis."

They ate a couple of sandwiches at the deli near the parking garage, then hailed another cab.

The ride back to the B and B proved a slow one, with the car crawling along in the traffic. While they sat at yet another clogged intersection, Mickey said, "Dan?"

"Uh-huh?"

"You never did tell me who phoned. The voice from the past."

He glanced at the divider, obviously assuring himself that it was shut, but then simply sat staring at the back of the front seat.

She didn't know whether she should press him or not, because it was clearly a subject he'd rather not talk about.

Just as she decided to let it go, he said, "It was my father."

"Oh."

His father. With whom he'd told her he didn't keep in touch.

As badly as she was dying to ask what the call had been about, she didn't let herself.

Eventually he said, "He was letting me know that my brother is getting early parole."

"Oh," she said again.

"And he thinks that, once Sean's out, the three of us should spend a few days together."

She waited, finally saying, "What do *you* think?"

He shook his head. "I don't know."

There were several beats of silence before he added, "I mean, I was planning on going to California for a while after Sean was released. I didn't expect it would be this soon, but that's not a problem. When you work on contract your schedule's pretty flexible.''

''So the problem,'' she said tentatively, after another silence, ''is that your father wants to be there, too.''

''Exactly.''

She covered his hand with hers, wishing she knew what to say. But it was hard to relate to his situation when she adored her father—her mother, as well—and enjoyed being with them.

''Was your childhood that unhappy?'' she asked at last.

He shrugged. ''In our neighborhood, nobody had model parents. Most of them smacked their kids around.

''My mom didn't,'' he elaborated. ''Just my dad. But it wasn't that so much as...well, we always knew he'd rather we didn't exist.''

''Oh, Dan,'' she murmured.

''I don't think he actually hated us. We were just in the way—noisy boys who irritated him when we were in the house and got in trouble when we weren't.

''We'd play baseball in the street and break a neighbor's window. Or one of us would have a fight at school and the principal would be on the phone to the old man. And we cost money, when he figured there were better things to spend it on. Beer, for example.

"But there's no point in talking about it," he added, shrugging again. "That's just the way he was. The way he is."

She felt like crying. Wished she could magically change his childhood. Realized that was impossible.

"You know when I resent him most?" Dan said. "Now, as an adult?"

"When?" she said softly.

"When I see a father really enjoying his children. Doing something with them because he wants to. And I think, man, if I ever had kids I'd try so damned hard with them…"

She hesitated, then said, "Do you think you ever will? Have kids, I mean?"

"No. How could I? You know what my life is like," he added, catching her gaze. "A woman would have to be crazy to take on a man like me."

Crazy in love, an imaginary voice whispered.

Mickey tried to pretend she hadn't heard it, but that was impossible. Just as impossible as the fact that she probably *was* crazy in love with Daniel O'Neill.

She couldn't tell him that, though, for a hundred different reasons. The main one being that what he'd just said was true.

She'd known it from the beginning. A woman would have to be crazy to take on a man like him.

So she said, "Why do you think your dad suddenly wants to get together?"

"I don't know. I guess it could be that he's lonely. My parents didn't have the greatest marriage, but they were company for each other. And since my mother died…''

''Could he be trying to make amends? Because he's sorry he wasn't a better father?''

''That might be a possibility. I just don't know.''

''So what are you going to do?''

Dan shook his head. ''I don't know that, either.''

She waited a few moments, then said, ''Would it have been hard for him to phone you?''

''Yeah, I'm sure it was.''

''Then…for him to have made the effort…''

''You're saying I should go along with his idea?''

''No. I'm just saying that if it was hard for him, and you reject it…well, he might never try again.''

After a short silence, Dan said, ''I'll have to do some thinking before I call him back.''

The hesitation in his voice made her long to take him in her arms and never let him go.

The feeling only grew stronger as they rode the rest of the way to the B and B.

By the time she was following him up the stairs, her heart was hammering and all she could think about was being completely alone with him again.

About touching him. And kissing him. And making love with him.

He'd obviously been thinking along the same lines, because the moment they were inside their room he pulled her close and kissed her hungrily. His body, pressing hard against hers, made her forget about everything else—until his cell phone began to ring.

He took his arms from around her with such obvious reluctance that it made her feel wonderful. Then he dug the phone out of his pocket and glanced at the call display.

"I'll have to speak to Lydia about her lousy timing," he muttered before answering.

A moment later, he nodded to Mickey, silently telling her that Lydia had the information they'd been waiting for.

"Who is he?" she asked the moment he clicked off.

"His name is Jake Remmington, and he works in the computer department of Carringsly, Ness and Blanchard."

"That's a law firm," she said, recognizing the name.

"Uh-huh. One of the biggest in the country. Branches in major cities from coast to coast.

"I've got to check on something," he added, punching in a number.

"Ken, it's Dan," he said into the phone a moment later. "I need to talk to Billy."

Mickey held her breath, certain that Dan thought he had the puzzle solved—and praying he really did.

As badly as she'd wanted her front-page story, as badly as she still wanted it, constantly fearing for her life was taking a serious toll on her nerves.

"Billy," he said. "What's your lawyer's name? The one who drew up your will."

He jotted that information down, then said, "What firm is he with?"

After a few seconds that seemed like an hour, he gave Mickey a thumbs-up, saying, "Carringsly, Ness and Blanchard. Yeah, I've heard of them. And where's the original copy of the will? Their New York office or in L.A.?

"L.A., huh?" he said after another couple of seconds.

"Yeah, I *do* think I'm onto something. I'll get back to you as soon as I know for sure."

He stuck his phone away, saying, "This has got to be it. The paper document might be in L.A., but there'll be a computer file of that will. And if Jake Remmington managed to get at it...well, he must have. Anything else would be just too big a coincidence. That means he and Maria know exactly how much money her daughter would get if Billy died. And until Kathryn's an adult, Maria would basically have control of it."

"And it's really enough to commit murder for?"

"Mickey, not only would she be on easy street, she'd never have to worry about Billy deciding he was tired of supporting her. Or worry that maybe, given the crazy ideas he comes up with, he might sometime decide he wants custody of his daughter."

"Then...it's over? We know she and Remmington hired Turk, and now we go to the police?"

She glanced at her laptop, thinking she'd have to take both it and her camera along this time around. She'd want to get her story off to the *Post* the minute everything was wrapped up.

But Dan was saying, "Well, no, it's not *quite* over.

What we've got at this point is mostly just a theory. Even if it's right, which I'm sure it is, the cops can't arrest someone without more than that.

"And the problem is, while they were trying to get enough hard proof that we're right, our friend Turk would still be walking around loose. Our own, personal, ticking bomb."

"You're saying *we* have to get them the hard proof, aren't you," she said uneasily.

DAN FOUND a parking space down the street from Maria Rosemount's brownstone, then sat gazing into the rearview mirror until Mickey said, "If Turk *is* still following us, how can we possibly not have spotted him by now?"

"Because he's that good."

And he *was* still following them. Either that or Dan's gut was lying to him, which it rarely did.

However, this would all be over soon. And he'd sure as hell be a lot happier after it was.

He reached over and gave Mickey's hand a squeeze.

When she shot him an anxious smile he wanted to just put the car back into gear and drive for a thousand miles.

That wasn't an impulse he could act on, though. He'd never quit an assignment partway through before, and he certainly didn't intend to now.

He was going to insure that Turk spent the rest of his life behind bars, where he'd be no threat to Mickey or Billy or anyone else.

Besides, if he and Mickey did just take off, what would they do once they got those thousand miles away? Spend the rest of their lives making love?

That was an incredibly appealing idea, but it was hardly realistic. In actuality, when they *did* get this wrapped up…

He mentally shook his head, not wanting to think about Mickey going home.

Oh, somewhere in the near future he'd be in the San Francisco area to spend that time with his brother.

The old man hadn't said exactly when Sean would be getting out, and it might be better to wait until after his father had been and gone—he was still mulling that in the back of his mind—but while he was there he'd see Mickey.

After that, though…

"Let's go," he said, opening his door and trying to banish the thought that, after his trip to California, he might never see her again.

They walked the few hundred yards down the block and buzzed Maria's apartment.

Just like the first time, the front curtains moved before she said, "Yes?"

"It's Dan O'Neill," he told her, "I'm sorry to bother you again, but we need a few more minutes. Something new has come up that we have to ask you about."

There was a silence, then she said "Sure," and buzzed them into the foyer. When she opened her apartment door, a little girl was clinging to her leg.

"You must be Kathryn," Mickey said, smiling and crouching down to kid level.

Kathryn hid her face.

"Come on in," Maria said.

She closed the door behind them and led the way into the living room, Kathryn holding tightly to her hand and not looking at them.

Dan cleared his throat.

When Maria glanced his way, he nodded meaningfully toward the child.

"Honey," she said, scooping the girl up into her arms, "I just have to talk to these people for two seconds, so how about if you finish coloring that picture of the puppies."

She carried her daughter down the hall and left her in what he assumed was her bedroom, then walked rapidly back to the living room.

"Well?" she said, rubbing her bare arms and eyeing him warily.

There was no point in beating around the bush, so he simply said, "We know about Jake Remmington."

Her composure vanished and he could see her desperately trying to decide what she should say.

"Jake Remmington," was all she finally went with, managing to sound as if she'd never heard the name before.

"Your friend," he said. "The fellow who was here earlier. The one who got hold of a copy of Billy's will so you could see if Kathryn was mentioned."

Again she clearly wasn't sure which way to jump.

"Billy told me she was included in it," she said at last.

Dan nodded, although Billy had said that he'd never told her anything about the will.

"But...well, you can't always believe what Billy says," she added. "So I wanted to check. Just to be sure."

He eyed her evenly for a moment, then said, "Look, Maria, we know you paid for the contract on Billy."

"No," she snapped without a second's hesitation. "I didn't."

"Yes, you did. *You* hired Turk."

When she realized they knew the hit man's identity, her face went pale.

"The only thing we aren't clear about," he continued, "is how you got hooked up with Remmington. How you found him and convinced him to—"

"No, that's not how it was!"

He took a long, slow breath, telling himself to lower the volume.

Maria might have arranged for the contract on Billy, but she hardly represented the direct threat that Turk did. Neither to Billy, nor to Mickey and him.

Which meant the critical thing was to convince her to cooperate. And the way to do that wasn't by getting her more upset. It was by making her see why joining ranks with them was in her own best interest.

If he could do that, there was far more chance

Turk would find himself in custody—soon, before anyone ended up dead.

"Look," he said quietly, digging out a business card and handing it to her. "I don't actually work for Billy. I work for Risk Control International, which is a company that occasionally gets involved with NYPD cases."

When she didn't look as if she was catching his drift, he said, "What I'm telling you is that RCI has a good reputation with the police, so the version of the story I give them is the one they'll believe.

"After that, you'd have a hard time convincing them of anything different. So you'd be smart to tell us exactly what the truth is right now."

"I'm not saying another word without a lawyer present," Maria muttered.

He shrugged. "Fine. But I've got no interest in talking to a lawyer, so Mickey and I will just head off to see the police. And we'll tell them that you went to Jake Remmington and had him get you a copy of Billy's will. And that once you'd seen how much your daughter would inherit if Billy was dead, you hired a hit man to take care of that for you."

When Maria simply stared at the floor, he said, "You *do* realize you'll be charged with attempted murder, don't you? Or with murder, if Turk actually does kill Billy?"

She looked at him then, and said, "I *didn't* go to Jake Remmington. And I *didn't* hire this Turk person. Jake did. And he came to me. Killing Billy was his idea, not mine."

''Oh?'' Dan said skeptically.

''It was! Everyone in the world—including Jake—knows that Kathryn is Billy's daughter, thanks to the pictures of Billy and me in the tabloids when I was pregnant. And the stories about me after Kathryn was born.

''In any event, Jake's...well, he's some sort of computer genius. I wouldn't be surprised if he could hack into the Pentagon's system, so getting a copy of Billy's will from the company he works for was child's play. And once he'd done that he contacted me. He showed me the will and said that for a portion of the inheritance he'd arrange for Billy's death.

''I...at first I said no—that I didn't want anything to do with the idea. But then he started in about how, just because this current will left Kathryn a fortune, it didn't guarantee she'd ever get it. He pointed out that Billy could change his mind a few years down the road. Or next week, for that matter. And knowing Billy...

''Anyway, Jake said that, as her mother, I'd have control over the money until she came of age. And that I could pay him off over time, so that if anyone ever checked there wouldn't be this one big suspicious amount. It was all *his* plan,'' she added. ''He looked after hiring the hit man. I wasn't involved in anything. I—''

''You agreed to pay him a share of Kathryn's inheritance after Billy was dead,'' Dan interrupted. ''As far as the law is concerned, that makes you every bit as guilty.''

Maria considered that, looking about two seconds away from total panic.

Finally she swallowed hard a couple of times and said, "Okay. There has to be a better option than getting charged with attempted murder. If you were me, what would you do?"

"Make a deal with the police. Do you know a good criminal lawyer?"

When she shook her head, he said, "Well, you want someone good negotiating for you. I have an associate who'll be able to get somebody fast but we should get moving on it right away.

"I can call the cops if you'd like. Arrange for a couple of detectives from Manhattan North Homicide to come and take a statement from you. And I can see about getting a lawyer here, too.

"Once the police have talked to you, they'll put out an APB on Turk. And as long as they get to him before he gets to Billy…well, a smart lawyer should be able to cut you a really good deal. Especially when you'll have voluntarily turned state's evidence. That always counts for a lot."

"Okay," she murmured. "Then that's what I'll do. But I can't have the police coming here and questioning me in front of Kathryn."

"Talking to them here would be best," he said, thinking that if Turk really was out there watching…

"No," she said firmly. "That's not going to happen."

He considered pressing the issue but decided

against it. The most important thing was that she didn't change her mind about talking to the cops.

''All right, then we'll go to the precinct,'' he said. ''And,'' he added, digging out his phone and punching in Lydia's number, ''I'll get on to somebody right now about a lawyer. We'll have one meet us there.''

Maria nodded. ''While you're doing that, I'll call my mother. She doesn't live far, so as long as she's home we can drop Kathryn off on the way.''

CHAPTER EIGHTEEN

PARKED DOWN THE STREET from Maria Rosemount's brownstone for the second time that day, Turk was feeling a whole lot better about things.

While O'Neill and the woman had been having lunch, he'd called his friend Louie—the one who'd do pretty much anything if the price was right—and made some arrangements. Now, instead of sitting here in his own car, he was sitting in one that Louie had heisted.

Hell, the guy should have been the star of that movie, *Gone in Sixty Seconds.* And he really was a good man to know.

He'd even changed the plates, so that when the owner reported the theft the cops would be looking for different tags. Not that the NYPD had much time to worry about stolen cars.

But they *would* be interested in this particular car if he decided to do a drive-by.

Suddenly, the door of Maria's place opened and it wasn't just O'Neill and the reporter who came out.

Maria and a kid—had to be her daughter—were with them.

Turk swore to himself. Unless he wanted to leave

witnesses he'd have to whack all four of them, and he sure didn't like that idea.

Taking out two people wasn't a major deal. Not even when he was certain that O'Neill and Michelle Westover were both carrying.

Of course, she was loaded down with not only her camera bag and purse, but a laptop, as well, so she wouldn't be able to get at her gun quickly.

Plus, he'd have the element of surprise. That counted for a lot.

Four people, though, even if one was a kid.

Shit, you started trying to whack four people at once, odds were high that you'd find yourself in trouble.

He could only hit one of them at a time, and the minute he started shooting they'd all be diving for cover.

Angrily he eyed the cars parked along the street. They were lined up practically bumper to bumper, which made for an awful lot of cover.

And if he didn't get both O'Neill and Westover on the first try it would turn into a damn shooting match out here, which would have half the neighbors on the phone to the cops.

He thought for a minute, trying to figure out if there was any way of making this work. He wanted to be rid of those two right here and now.

But he was going to have to resign himself to waiting a little longer. Here and now would be just too risky.

Muttering under his breath, he watched them all pile into O'Neill's rental.

WHILE THEY HEADED up Central Park West, with Maria sitting as stiffly as a statue in the back seat and Kathryn engaged in a whispered conversation with her doll, Mickey began trying to figure out how she was going to get a picture of Maria.

When Jake Remmington had been leaving Maria's place, she'd shot half a dozen of him, so she was covered there. But the *Post* editors would want photos of *both* people who'd conspired to have Billy murdered.

The problem was, when she took her camera out of its case, Maria would want to know what was going on. And admitting that she was a photojournalist and needed a picture to accompany an article about the contract on Billy's life... Well, Maria would likely try to trash the camera.

Of course, experienced hard-news journalists wouldn't spend a nanosecond worrying about how Maria would react. They'd simply click off a bunch of shots—preferably, with the precinct building as background.

So was that what *she'd* do?

She guessed she'd have to.

But why was she worrying about it, anyway? Maria had put a contract out on someone's life, for Pete's sake.

Oh, maybe she honestly hadn't come up with the idea. That was believable.

She'd certainly gone along with it, though, which meant she deserved whatever press she got.

"Mommy?" Kathryn said. "Am I gonna have my dinner at Grandma's?"

Suddenly Mickey realized what was bothering her. It wasn't really Maria's feelings she was concerned about, it was Kathryn's.

The poor little girl had a father she saw for a couple of hours, two or three times a year, and now her mother was probably going to end up in prison.

She wondered whether Kathryn was old enough that her friends would see the media coverage and tease her. The *Post*'s exclusive would be the first of it and...

She told herself not to even think about that, because she was only doing her job. And she shouldn't have the slightest hesitation about that. Unless...

Unless she was actually too soft to cover hard news.

She firmly assured herself she wasn't. Besides, if for some reason she didn't get the shots she still needed, the paper could always run a file picture.

As Maria had said, she'd been hot news for a while after she'd given birth to Billy Brent's daughter, so coming up with a photograph of her wouldn't be tough.

Dan turned off Central Park West onto one of the cross streets, then glanced into the rearview at Maria, and said, "What number?"

"It's the third building on the right," she told him.

As Mickey's thoughts returned to the moment, she

noted that although they hadn't driven far, the character of the neighborhood had changed considerably.

The brownstones on this street were well maintained, but not impressive looking. Obviously, they'd originally been built as multidwelling, working or middle-class homes.

"I'll just run in with Kathryn," Maria said as Dan pulled up in the No Parking zone out front.

"We'll come with you," he told her.

Right, Mickey thought. It was well worth risking a ticket, because if they let Maria out of their sight she might decide she didn't want to go to the police after all.

"Wait a sec," Dan said as she reached for her door handle. "I'm not trying to make you nervous, but we should get inside as quickly as possible."

"Why?"

"I'll explain later. Do you have a front door key?"

"No, but my mother will be watching for me. She'll buzz us right in."

"Good," he said. Then he checked both ways along the street.

Mickey could feel adrenaline pumping through her. Surely, though, nothing was going to happen now. Not when all of this was so close to being over.

"Okay," Dan said. "Let's go."

They climbed out of the car and hurried up the steps—Kathryn in her mother's arms—and sure enough, the buzzer started sounding before they reached the front door.

Once it had closed behind them and they were

safe, Mickey was tempted to take a picture of Maria holding Kathryn.

She knew she should, that it would make a great human-interest shot to accompany her story. On the other hand, her piece was about a murder contract on Billy Brent. It had nothing to do with his daughter.

Besides, Maria was already incredibly upset and Kathryn was shy with strangers. So she doubted she could make herself start shooting pictures if she tried, which didn't do anything to help her concern that maybe she really *was* too soft to cover hard news.

If that was true, she'd been deluding herself from the day the *Post* had hired her.

''I WANNA GO WITH YOU,'' Kathryn insisted.

''No, you stay here with Grandma,'' Maria told her. ''I'll be back soon.''

As she gave her daughter a big hug, Mickey glanced at Dan, wondering whether Maria would really be back anytime within the next ten years.

She'd had no chance to ask him what, specifically, would happen to Maria, but she was pretty sure the police detectives wouldn't simply take her statement and then let her go.

Not even if Lydia came up with a *really* sharp lawyer. Not when they were talking party to an attempted murder.

However, at least it was only *attempted.* And as Dan had said, it would remain that way as long as the cops got to Turk before he got to Billy.

"You be a good girl while I'm gone," Maria said.

"Maria," her mother murmured, "can't you at least tell me what's going on?"

"Not right now. We're in a hurry."

She kissed the top of Kathryn's head, then turned and practically ran out of the apartment.

As Mickey and Dan followed her down the stairs, Mickey tried telling herself that good reporters were hard-nosed about their work. They didn't let their emotions get in the way.

Yet she just couldn't help wishing that Maria had told Jake Remmington to take a hike when he'd come along with his stupid proposal. Then there'd have been no contract on Billy and Maria wouldn't be facing the likelihood of a prison term.

But if there'd been no contract on Billy, Mickey Westover would never have met Daniel O'Neill. He wouldn't have been at Billy's retreat, lying in wait for Turk.

And if she'd never met Dan...

Lord, maybe that would have been better than *having* met him, because once she went home, she was going to miss him so incredibly much that she didn't want to even imagine how horrible she'd feel.

When they reached the front door, Maria turned toward them and said, "Are you certain this is the best thing I can do?"

"Absolutely," Dan assured her. "And it'll turn out a lot better than you think."

He opened the door and took a moment to check the street, then began hustling Maria and Mickey down the steps. They'd almost reached the sidewalk when Mickey caught a motion with her peripheral vision.

Just as she turned her head, the air exploded with a rapid-fire series of shots.

All at once Maria was screaming and Dan was half dragging them between two parked cars, yelling "Get down!"

As her knees hit the pavement, Mickey felt a bullet whiz by her head and heard it ricochet off a car.

Her ears were ringing, her heart was pounding; she'd never been so terrified.

Then, as abruptly as it had begun, the shooting stopped.

Dan already had his gun drawn and whispered that Mickey should get hers out.

"Stay here and don't move," he added. "But if you see him, shoot to kill."

As he began inching his way along the side of a car, Maria was clutching her thigh and sobbing that she'd been shot. Blood was slowly turning the creamy fabric of her skirt red.

"You're going to be okay," Mickey whispered. "I know how badly it must hurt, but you're going to be okay.

"Your mother will have heard the shooting," she added, digging into her purse for the semiautomatic. "She'll call the police."

Her hands were trembling so badly that she took forever to get the gun out.

By the time she had, Dan had disappeared from sight.

She half thought she should go after him, but he'd told her not to move. And if Turk came this way…

She remained crouched beside Maria, desperately wishing she at least knew which direction she should be pointing her gun. If Turk did come this way, would he be on the sidewalk or the street?

That question had barely formed in her mind when there was another explosion of gunfire followed by a deathly silence.

One second…two…three…

No noise except the hammering of her heart and Maria's whimpering.

Trying to prevent an image of Dan lying dead from forming in her mind, she eased her way toward the passenger side of the car.

She was aware of a siren in the distance now, but if Dan had been shot…

"Mickey?" he called. "Everything's all right."

The sound of his voice was such a relief that she almost burst into tears.

When she pushed herself to her feet and looked along the block, Turk was lying, bleeding but conscious, on the pavement. Dan stood a few yards away, his gun aimed at Turk.

"Hey," he said, glancing at her, "I can hear the police on the way. So if you want to get any front-page pictures of a hit man, you'd better grab your camera."

THE COFFEE IN THE Internet Café was far from excellent, but Mickey had a third cup while she waited for Dan.

After they'd finished giving their statements to the detectives at Manhattan North Homicide, he'd left her here to write up the final version of her story while he'd gone to "see about a few things."

Since the ambulance attendants had said that neither Maria nor Turk had life-threatening wounds, she doubted he'd gone to the hospital to check on them.

More likely, he'd wanted to find out how Maria's lawyer had made out with the plea bargaining.

Glancing at her watch, she wondered how much longer he'd be. She'd sent her article and photographs off into the blue not more than half an hour ago, and already had a message back about them.

She looked at the screen of her laptop, reading the words for the millionth time.

"Excellent work!" it said. And it had come from the senior news editor at the *Post.*

Whenever the screen saver appeared, she moved the mouse to bring that message up again.

Excellent work!

And the only physical damage it had entailed was to her knees. They'd gotten skinned and bruised when she'd hit the pavement.

But those were very minor injuries compared to what might have been.

Taking another sip of coffee, she reflected that she'd done exactly what she'd set out to do—gotten an exclusive story that was front-page news.

She'd scooped every other reporter in the world.

So why wasn't she out dancing in the street?

She bumped the mouse again, aware the answer to that one was only too easy. Tomorrow she'd be flying home. Alone. Which wasn't a dancing-in-the-street prospect.

Maybe she *hadn't* been taken with Daniel O'Neill when they'd first met, and maybe she *had* figured he was the worst marriage material imaginable, but something he'd said had started her thinking she might have been wrong about that.

"If I ever had kids," he'd told her, "I'd try so damn hard with them..."

At any rate, somewhere along the way—she couldn't pinpoint exactly where—she'd realized that she'd fallen so hard she wanted to spend the rest of her life with him.

That wasn't going to happen, though.

She'd known from the beginning that he wasn't the sort of man who'd make a "forever" commitment. But recognizing the fact didn't make the idea of living without him any easier to handle.

She sensed that he was standing behind her at the exact moment he rested his hands on her shoulders and said, "Sorry I took so long."

She didn't know which she loved more—his touch or the sound of his voice.

"It's okay," she said, turning to look up at him and thinking that there was a whole long list of things she loved about him.

"See what I got?" she added, gesturing toward the screen.

He read the message and smiled. "Hey, that's terrific. You must be thrilled."

She nodded, adding his smile to her list. "I don't think they even cared that I didn't send a picture of Maria. How is she, by the way?"

"Good. As the medics said, it was just a flesh wound. So she probably won't even be in the hospital overnight."

"And when she's discharged?"

"Things are going to be better than she had any right to hope. Lydia obviously came up with an *extremely* good lawyer. But let's get out of here," he suggested, picking up her camera case.

She closed her laptop and followed him out into the early evening.

"Should we get some dinner?" he asked. "There's an okay-looking restaurant just down the block."

"Sure. Tell me the details about Maria, though."

"Well, the lawyer Lydia found is still negotiating terms with a couple of homicide detectives, but they've already agreed that she won't go to prison. They'll settle for some time under house arrest."

"Isn't it...surprising that she'll get off so easy?"

Dan smiled again. "Didn't I say the lawyer was extremely good? And aside from that, the fact she gave the cops both Jake Remmington and Turk made them really happy. They figure Turk's responsible for several of their unsolved cases—that they'll ultimately be able to charge him with more than just attempted murder.''

Mickey nodded, not sure she should be glad that Maria was getting off so lightly.

Should be or not, though, she *was* glad.

Maybe that was mostly for Kathryn's sake, but she didn't suppose the *why* mattered much.

They reached the restaurant—a cozy little Italian place—and put their conversation on hold until they'd been seated.

Once the maître d' was gone, Mickey asked, ''Did you call Billy?''

''Uh-huh.''

''And he said?''

''He wanted to know why it had taken me so damn long to sort things out.''

She laughed. ''You know, I *really* want to meet that man. I just can't believe he's as awful as everyone makes him out to be.''

''Believe it. And you will meet him, won't you? I mean, he still owes you an interview. Or has the *Post* already promoted you out of Arts and Entertainment?''

''No. Not yet.''

''Well, it'll happen.''

When she didn't reply, Dan said, ''Is something wrong?''

''Oh...I don't know exactly how to explain it, but now that I'll probably get offered what I wanted, I'm not as sure I want it.''

''Because?''

"Maybe I'm just not a hard-news kind of person. Taking those pictures of Turk, lying in the street, staring at me with utter hatred in his eyes... Well, even though he'd tried to kill us I felt kind of..."

She shrugged, finding it hard to put her feelings into words. "I guess part of the problem is that even though I've always thought I should be doing more significant stories, I actually enjoy celebrity interviews and things like that.

"They involve talking to people who want me to write about them and want me to take their picture, which is nice. Whereas this story about Billy and Turk and Maria and... Well, there were a lot of things about covering it that I didn't really like."

"Almost getting killed, for example?"

That made her smile. "Yes. For example."

A waiter materialized with menus. As he left, Dan said, "I also called my father."

"Oh?"

"I wanted to know exactly when Sean was being released, which turns out to be in a couple of weeks. And I told him I thought the three of us *should* spend some time together.

"I'm not too optimistic about how it'll go, but...you never know."

"Right. You never do," she said, silently telling her pulse to stop racing.

Dan might be coming to San Francisco in only a couple of weeks, but he hadn't said he wanted to see her while he was there.

And even if he did, probably the smartest thing she could do would be to tell him no.

When she was with him, she seemed to grow crazier about him by the minute. So wouldn't seeing him again only make the eventual hurting worse?

"Mickey?" he said, reaching across the table and taking her hands in his.

Her heart began beating even faster. "Yes?"

"Now that this assignment's wrapped up, I was thinking I deserve some time off. And... How would you feel about seeing if we can *both* catch a flight to San Francisco tomorrow? About my spending the two weeks until Sean gets out, with you?"

She tried to remind herself that she'd be smart to tell him no, but couldn't get herself to say the word.

She wanted to be with him so badly she ached. Even if it was only for another couple of weeks.

"I think that would be great," she said softly.

He smiled again, looking so relieved that she realized he'd been afraid she might not like the idea.

Until this moment she wouldn't have believed Daniel O'Neill would ever be afraid of anything.

"Look," he said, "I know I shouldn't push...oh, hell, I just can't seem to shut up.

"Mickey, it's the last thing I'd have ever expected but I think I've...fallen in love with you."

She could feel herself grinning like an idiot, but she couldn't stop. "Me, too," she murmured.

"Well...terrific. That's really terrific."

Now *he* was grinning like an idiot.

"So, I've been thinking...I know it's way too

soon to be saying anything, but if these...feelings between us turn out to be for real...and I just can't believe they won't... Well, there has to be some way of working things out so that we could be together." He swallowed hard, then added, "Permanently, I mean."

Oh, wow, she felt as if fireworks were going off and trumpets were sounding.

"Yes," she managed to say. "There are probably a whole lot of different ways we could work things out."

He nodded, saying, "See, I figure the main problem is that you wouldn't want any part-time sort of arrangement. And I don't *have* to live in Connecticut, but I'd still have to travel."

"Well, if you weren't away *too* much. I'm used to being on my own."

"I could do less traveling. And take as many assignments as possible in California."

"Uh-huh. That would be good."

Good? Merely *good?* Had her mind turned to mush?

"I mean, that would be wonderful, Dan."

"Hey," he said, still grinning, "do you want to forget about dinner for the moment? Get out of here?"

He dug a couple of bills out of his pocket and tossed them on the table, adding, "Go somewhere more private?"

"And fool around?" she teased.

"Yeah," he said. "That would be *wonderful.*"

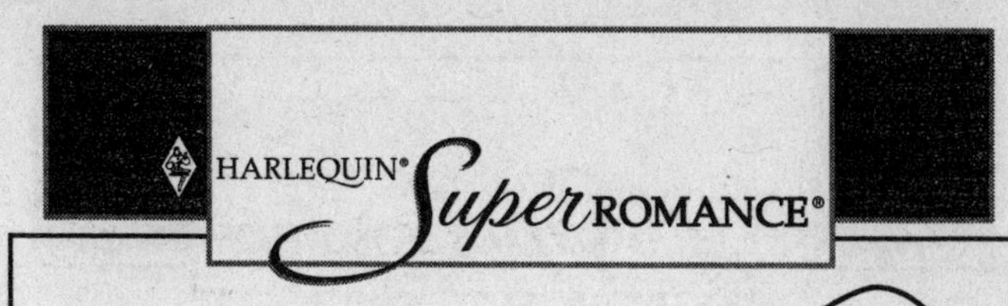
HARLEQUIN®
SuperROMANCE®

9 MONTHS LATER

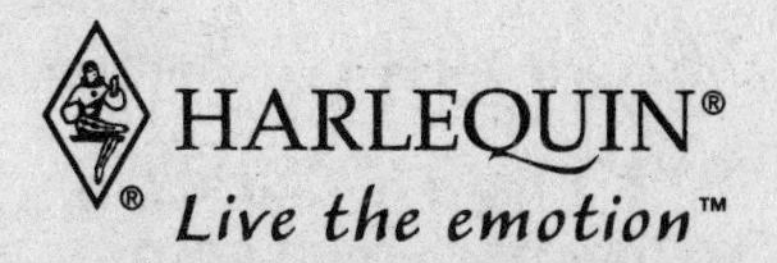
HARLEQUIN®
Live the emotion™